Accused:
A Tale of the Salem Witch Trials

by Jeani Rector

Accused:
A Tale of the Salem Witch Trials

by Jeani Rector

Wallowing in all kind of sin,
vile wretches lay secure:
The best of men had scarcely then
their Lamps kept in good ure.
Virgins unwise, who through disguise
amongst the best were number'd,
Had closed their eyes; yea, and the wise
through sloth and frailty slumber'd.

The Day of Doom
Michael Wigglesworth, Puritan Poet
(1631–1705)

Published by The Horror Zine Books

Bat art created by Riaan Marais

Cover and Interior Design By
Stephen James Price
www.BookLooksDesign.com

Published by The Horror Zine Books
www.thehorrorzine.com

Copyright 2013 by The Horror Zine Books. No part of this publication can be reproduced, stored in a retrieval system, or transmitted by any form or by any means, mechanical, digital, electronic, photocopying or recording, except for inclusion in a review, without permission in writing from Jeani Rector.

Except for historical circumstances, all contents in this book are works of fiction.

Artwork is legally purchased from istock.

Ergot:

"Ergot refers to a group of fungi of the genus *Claviceps*. The most prominent member of this group is *Claviceps purpurea*. This fungus grows on rye and related plants, and produces alkaloids that can cause ergotism in humans and other mammals who consume grains contaminated with its fruiting structure."
– Wikipedia

Symptoms of Ergotism:

"The neuropathic effects of ergot alkaloids may cause hallucinations and corresponding irrational behavior, muscle spasms, convulsions, coma, and even death."
– Wikipedia

Author's Note

There have been many theories as to what triggered the hysteria during the Salem Witch Trials in 1692 Massachusetts. This was an episode in America's early history that still fascinates the general public today. The Puritans' deviation from what would seem to be logical beliefs and normal human behavior has been the subject of numerous attempts to explain why. Why did this happen? How did it get so out of hand?

This book focuses upon the theory that tainted rye grain, infected with the ergot virus (which is a strong hallucinogen if ingested), may have been the original catalyst in an event of horrific magnitude.

Accused: A Tale of the Salem Witch Trials is a work of fiction, but it is based upon actual events in American history. I have tried to bring the reader directly into the times of 1692 Salem Town and Salem Village. There was an incredible amount of superstition which seems ludicrous by today's standards, but were the accepted beliefs at the time.

In this book, the speech of the characters is modern, and not the Olde English actually spoken in the 17th Century. This is done for the ease of the reader and to move the storyline along smoothly. In reality, the contrast of speech today and that which was spoken in Puritan times is so great that it could almost be considered a different language, even though technically it is not.

Almost all of the characters depicted in this account were real people that lived during the late 17th Century in Salem Town and Salem Village. Tituba and John Indian were real. Despite the fact that she confessed to a capital offense through coercion and was a slave, Tituba was never executed. She was sent to jail and was surprisingly later released, but there is no record of what happened to her afterwards.

Another real person was Reverend Samuel Parrish. On June 18, 1689, the village agreed to hire Samuel Parris as their minister for £66 annually, "one third part in money and the other two third parts in provisions" and the use of the parsonage. In Chapter Three, William's conversation about Reverend Parris' personal history before he came to Salem Village is accurate.

Reverend Parris is portrayed to be an emotional monster in this book, and while perhaps exaggerated, the reality is that Parris was not an ideal spiritual leader because he was concerned about money, status, and was a very paranoid individual. He was definitely over-zealous with his religious beliefs to the extent that he harbored fanatical ideas about Satan, and therefore was a danger to the community. The deaths of innocent people were the result.

However, it is a creative liberty of fiction to depict Reverend Parris' specific words and behaviors towards Ruth Putnam, Abigail Williams and Tituba Indian outside of the trials, and there is no historical mention of a mulatto child, so these things were made up to move the plot of this book along.

Abigail Williams and Betty Parrish were real, they were cousins, and they were the first participants in the witch mania. Abigail did indeed live in the Parrish household. I have made their ages a couple of years older than they really were at the time of the Salem Witch Trials.

William Porter was a real person, but much too young during the Witch Trials to be the William in this book, so his character could be considered fictional. Israel Porter was a real person.

Ruth Putnam is perhaps the only completely fictional character, invented to be a person who would see the events unfolding from her point of view.

It is a coincidence that many of the real people in this book had a last name that begins with the letter "P," but since the names in this book were indeed their real names, I was unable to change any of them. I hope that so many last names beginning with "P" does not confuse the reader.

Now about the history in this book: Salem was a hierarchical society in the late 1600s. Women of status were titled Mrs., but the women of lower social status were simply called Goody, short for "Goodwife."

Both women and children respected and revered the decisions of the men in the Puritan society without question, so the proactive personality of Ruth Putman in this book would be considered abnormal behavior for the times.

The abandonment of the child Dorcas Good (also known as Dorothy) really happened: the four-year-old girl was left to wander around the jail, pining for her mother who was imprisoned inside. Although little Dorcas was eventually also imprisoned, she was released after nine months, and sadly went insane afterwards.

Meanwhile, the mother Goody Good gave birth to another child while jailed. That newborn child died shortly after birth, inside the dungeon that was the jail.

Any references to jail breakouts in this book are invented, and that also applies to chase scenes, both written to add excitement to the plotline.

Now back to historical reality: there was no jury in the Salem Witch Trials. The magistrate, John Hathorne, acted more like a prosecutor than an impartial judge. Any testimony from the "witches" was to be ignored and argued against, and it was accepted that any defense they offered would be lies. Many years later, Hathorne's grandson, author Nathaniel Hawthorne, added a "w" to his last name to distance himself from his grandfather because of the role he played in the Salem trials.

As unbelievable as it may seem by today's standards, some of the testimony at the witch trials described in this book was taken from actual trial transcripts. When you read trial testimony about such things as "yellow birds," being pinched, and being forced to "sign Satan's book," those words were actually uttered in various trials.

The testimony from the children, despite the ridiculousness of its content, was considered as the gospel truth, because children were thought to be innocents and therefore "God could speak through them."

Yet were they so innocent? Perhaps ergot poisoning may or may not have begun the witch trials, but political power and land grabs most certainly fueled them.

Perhaps the testimonies of the children were influenced by adults who saw this as an easy method to get rid of enemies: simply accuse them of witchcraft. You want to buy fertile land near a source of water very cheaply? Accuse the current owner of witchcraft and then simply buy the property for a very low price afterwards, once the desired property is vacated.

Contrary to common belief, the accused witches in Salem Village were not burned at the stake. All were hanged, with the exceptions of those who died while incarcerated. Another exception was the fate of Giles Cory, who was made to lie flat on the ground and had a board placed upon his chest. Rocks were then piled upon the board. Giles Cory was crushed to death.

The list of innocent people accused of witchcraft and were hanged is below, in alphabetical order.

Bridget Bishop
George Burroughs
Martha Carrier
Martha Cory
Mary Easty
Sarah Good
Elizabeth Howe
George Jacobs
Susannah Martin
Rebecca Nurse
Alice Parker
Mary Parker
John Proctor
Ann Pudeator
Wilmot Redd

ACCUSED: A TALE OF THE SALEM WITCH TRIALS

Margaret Scott
Samuel Wardwell
Sarah Wildes
John Willard

The names of those that died in jail are listed below, again in alphabetical order.

Sarah Good's newborn baby
(born and died in the jail dungeon)
Lydia Dustin
Ann Foster
Sarah Osborne
Roger Toothaker

The book titled *Memorable Providences Relating to Witchcrafts and Possessions*, written by Boston minister Cotton Mather in 1689, was used as an instruction manual about how to persecute (and prosecute) suspected witches. The trials and events of 1692 escalated to a horrific level, and were only halted by the interference of Sir William Phipps, who at the time was the governor of Massachusetts.

The Puritans were a deeply religious people, and that is reflected in this book. However, any religious beliefs or superstitions portrayed in this book do not reflect my own personal beliefs. The same thing applies to any prejudices.

In modern times, religion has a valuable place in society, but so does science. Let's hope that today, religion and science will not be at odds against each other, but instead can find a way to co-exist and respect one another.

Preface

The spores traveled, unbidden and undetected, carried by insects that navigated between separate fields of rye. The bees and flies were attracted by the fetid-smelling sticky substance the toxic fungus produced for just this purpose. Spread across fields by insects, the spores found their way into new rye grasses, where they embedded themselves into the ovaries of the previously healthy plants.

There the Ergot of Rye fungus continued its parasitic growth cycle. It began consuming some of the healthy tissue of the rye grain and then replaced that with its own cells. In so doing, the ergot eventually ripened to produce a dark, dense, hard mass that somewhat resembled normal rye seed, but it was larger and darker-colored. Some of the purplish-black ergot sclerotia fell to the ground, there to repeat the life cycle in the next growing season.

But during that late summer of 1691, many grains of ergot fungus were harvested right along with the normal kernels of the rye plants.

This type of ergot was called *Claviceps purpurea*, and it produced a toxin that, if ingested, could induce seizures, convulsions, contractions of the tongue, pains in the limbs, and in extreme cases, hallucinations.

That growing season, the weather had been unusually damp and cool; ideal conditions for ergot to flourish. And flourish it did in the tiny Massachusetts farming community of Salem Village, located directly alongside Salem Town.

Once harvested, the infected rye grain was stored in the barns, because wheat was still plentiful in fall, and wheat was the preferred diet of the Puritans.

The ergot fungus patiently waited in the barns, its neuro-toxin lying undisturbed until the winter when the people of Salem Village would have a need to mill the rye into flour. That need arrived in the beginning of 1692.

When the Puritans baked rye bread, they provided the loaves containing the ergot toxin to their families.

Chapter One

"I know when you're going to die."

Ruth looked at the twelve-year-old girl who was speaking, trying to determine how to react to Abigail's words. It was cold, very cold outside where the three girls stood by the back door of the recently white-washed Parris house. That February in the new year of 1692 had blown into Salem Village with a mean spirit. The three girls huddled together for warmth, and also because they were whispering secrets.

"You have no way of knowing when I'll die," Ruth finally said, pulling her woolen cloak tighter around her shoulders. "That's only for God to know."

"Abigail knows," Betty Parris whispered. Betty was ten and always appeared very conscious of the fact that she was two years younger than her cousin, who lived with her family.

Ruth looked again at Abigail Williams, noticing how some of the girl's dark hair escaped the severe bun tucked under the winter cowl. The wayward strands of hair were blown about in the biting wind. She observed Abigail's face, taking in the girl's sharp features which included small, dark eyes that shined with intelligence. Yet it was Abigail's demeanor that unsettled Ruth the most; the girl rarely met people's eyes directly with her own, and she often behaved in a secretive, feral manner.

"Okay, Abigail," Ruth said with undisguised skepticism, "just how would you know when I'm going to die? I'm only seventeen, so I'm thinking I have a lot of time left."

Abigail's dark eyes narrowed. "Maybe you do have time, or maybe you don't. Not only can I tell you about *that*, but I know other things too. You're a Putnam. I've heard gossip about your family. I know a lot of things about you Putnams."

"She knows, she knows!" Betty said, hopping from one foot to the other to fend off the chill of the wind.

Deep in thought, Ruth studied the Parris house for a distraction. The gusts had piled the snow against the clapboards of the staunch, severe building. It was a dwelling so simple in its design that even though it contained two stories and an attic, it was sided with plain wooden boards all the way from the roof to the ground upon which it sat. The house was a huge square, straight, and without ornament. Too new of a building to have turned gray with weather, the Parris house was a blinding white, so freshly painted that there was no contrast between the house and the heavy snow piled against its base.

"Be quiet, Betty," Ruth said. She felt justified in her chastisement, as not only did her age give her an advantage over the other two, but also because Ruth was aware that she was indeed a Putnam. And members of the Putnam family had tremendous social status in Salem Village, so much that the elder Putnams were always addressed as Mr. and Mrs., not the Goodman and Goodwife titles given to those of low social status. And certainly the elder Putnams were never called "Goody," which was the abridged version of Goodman and Goodwife, and signified the lowest social status possible.

Ruth realized that she should probably give Betty some respect, since Betty was a Parris, and Reverend Parris was the minister of Salem Village. But Ruth found herself annoyed by both Betty and Abigail.

Turning away from Betty, Ruth focused her attention back upon Abigail. "Of course you know a lot of things about my family. Everyone knows my father. He owns the most farmland in all the Village," she said, then waited for a response. When none appeared to be materializing from Abigail, Ruth relented to her curiosity and asked, "All right…what do you know about my family? What have you heard?"

"Since my uncle is the minister in this Village, all sorts of people come to call," Abigail spoke slowly, as though she wanted to make the attention she was receiving last. The effect was there: the other two girls leaned forward to hear. All three wore cloaks, hand muffs, heavy woolen socks and tightly buttoned shoes. Ruth pulled her cowl away from her ears in order to better hear, because Abigail spoke softly, yet with a voice that held an underlying current of unpleasantness.

"Sometimes I sit at the top of the stairs at night to listen to what the grownups downstairs are talking about," Abigail continued.

"When?" Betty interrupted, obviously intrigued.

Abigail looked at her younger cousin with scorn on her face. "After you go to sleep, silly. You'd be too noisy to sit on the stairs with me and then someone would find out. That'd get us a whipping for sure."

She turned back to Ruth and began again. "Two nights ago, your father was over to our house. Uncle Parris told your father that since you've no marriage prospects, you should be sent to our house for awhile so you'd learn to keep house and cook. Since my aunt has been sick for so long, my uncle said it would benefit everybody for you to stay with us for a couple of months until my Aunt Parris gets better."

Ruth's heart sank at the news. She was conflicted with emotion; how could a person from her station in life come to this? On the surface, it was made to sound as though she would be an apprentice, but in reality, wasn't it servitude? What if Mrs. Parris didn't recover in any time soon?

And then there was something else to consider—the Parris household already had two servants, John Indian and his wife Tituba. Samuel Parris had given them "Indian" as last names simply because they were from the West Indies in the Caribbean. Puritan conventions deemed that everyone be given last names, and it appeared that Reverend Parris had not wanted to give the issue a lot of thought when he brought John and Tituba to the New World.

Was Ruth to serve the Parris household right alongside two

Negro slaves? Her father couldn't possibly agree to such a horrific plan.

Oh, it couldn't be true, it couldn't be true!

"You're lying," Ruth accused.

Abigail thrust her chin out, her dark eyes flashing. "Oh you think so? Well, let me tell you something else, Miss So-High-and-Mighty. Your father told my uncle that unless you marry, he feels no obligation to give you any parcels of his land. Your father said that his land can only stretch so far, and he has fine sons who need to inherit. So there, maybe your family isn't as rich as you think they are!"

"Stop it!" Ruth cried.

"Be quiet, or my father will hear," Betty warned.

"He's inside, so he can't hear us," Abigail said.

"You're lying," Ruth repeated, but she did lower her voice. "I don't care what you think you heard—it's not true. You're just jealous because I have a father and your father isn't alive any more. And I'm my father's favorite daughter. Anyway, what I really want to hear about is when you seem to think I'll die and see God in Heaven. Not that I'd believe you about *that*, either."

Abigail smiled for the first time, but her smile contained no humor. "I think that deep down, you believe what I'm saying."

Ruth wondered, *How can a twelve-year-old girl seem so confident, and so grown-up?* Suddenly she realized that she *did* believe the things Abigail was saying. Despite herself, Ruth couldn't conceal her morbid curiosity. "When?" she whispered. "When will I die?"

Abigail didn't speak for a moment, allowing the suspense to mount. Ruth waited in anguish, listening to the single tree in the yard creak and groan in protest as the winter wind bent the bare branches into submission. She was conscious of the stinging cold on her cheeks, but her nose was beyond feeling. She found herself wishing she were inside the house, any house, in front of a warm fire. But she knew that the things about which the girls were speaking should never, never be overheard by anyone's parents. That meant staying outdoors for safety's sake.

"I don't know yet, but I know how to find out." Abigail's words, when she finally spoke, both surprised and disappointed Ruth.

"What do you mean, you don't know yet?" Ruth was indignant. "You told me twice that you knew when I'm supposed to die."

"She knows, she knows!" Betty interjected again.

"Oh shut up." This time it was Abigail that snapped at the younger girl.

Then she turned to Ruth and said, "I'll have to show you. Your parents are still inside visiting with my uncle. Let's sneak upstairs, and I'll show you something magical that you'll want to see."

Unlike almost all other Village families, the Parris household wasn't full of children. This gave Abigail and Betty an almost unheard of amount of privacy. But Mrs. Parris had been sickly for many years, unable to conceive any more children after Betty, and recently she had become so ill that she was bedridden. Ruth shivered, not only from the cold wind of winter, but also because she knew that in the empty Parris household, sneaking about could be possible, and secrets kept by the children could be possible indeed.

She felt hesitant and unsettled, but then, almost as though it were someone else speaking, she heard herself agree to go upstairs to see whatever mystical thing Abigail had to show. But if it were as magical as Abigail had said, wouldn't it be going against the laws of God to view it? Everyone knew that magic was a sin.

Abigail turned around and strode towards the back door of the house with confident steps. Betty followed, trotting to keep up. Ruth remained behind, hesitating for just a moment longer because her heart suddenly thudded in her chest and her hands felt clammy inside the muffs she wore. The religious teachings in her life had taken hold, and Ruth felt an overpowering sense of guilt even though so far she had done nothing wrong.

Standing there with her feet in the snow, Ruth's mind quickly went over ways to justify why it would be all right to satisfy her curiosity. *After all*, she reasoned silently to herself, *Abigail is the niece of a minister so I'm sure she wouldn't do anything to go against God's Word. Besides, even if she did, I could put a stop to it at any time by simply walking away.*

So her mind became clear and finally Ruth jerked herself into mobility. Running after the other two girls, she reached them just as Abigail swung open the heavy wooden back door that led inside the Parris house.

The kitchen was large, and might have impressed Ruth had she not been used to even grander surroundings in her own household. The wooden planks of the floor were heavily varnished and were bare of rugs. Delectable fragrances were drifting from a large kettle simmering in the cookfire, and the scent seemed exotic, unlike the plain food which graced the Putnam table.

Another thing that Ruth noticed as she passed through the Parris kitchen was that the underlying smell was different. It smelled less of an odor of unwashed bodies that lingered in most houses, and more like the soaps that the Villagers made from animal fats. She realized that the kitchen must have been recently scrubbed. Perhaps Tituba Indian was unusually meticulous.

"Here's the stairway we'll take," Abigail pointed towards the narrow, white door located to the left of the cookstove. "These are the servants' stairs, so we can go upstairs without anyone knowing where we are."

"What if someone looks for us?" Ruth asked.

"They're in the parlor," Abigail explained, "and they're talking so much that it will be a while before they notice or even care where we are. But dinner will start pretty soon, so we'd better come downstairs before then."

It made sense to Ruth. She nodded.

Abigail started towards the servants' door, then stopped. "Wait," she said, "I need to get an egg."

Ruth didn't understand, but said nothing as she stood and watched Abigail turn around and reach into a linen-covered basket that was on a kitchen shelf. A large brown egg was retrieved from the basket and clutched it in the young girl's hand. The corners of her mouth upturned slightly as she once again made her way towards the servants' door.

Betty hopped after Abigail and again Ruth trailed behind. Once Abigail opened the door, Ruth could see that the passageway inside was narrow and dark.

Entering the servants' staircase, Ruth realized that the winter outerwear she wore hampered her efforts to navigate the steep stairwell. Each stair was at least twenty inches high and Ruth knew any false step could send her tumbling down into a heap at the base. She began carefully climbing, suddenly aware that she had been holding her breath. She released her breath and forced herself to try to relax, her fingers touching the walls on each side of the narrow staircase. Ruth had a very bad feeling about all this, but she was unable to suppress her curiosity. She found herself compelled to continue.

Finally the three girls reached the top, and Abigail opened the uppermost door. Light streamed into the stairwell. Ruth was relieved to see candles burning upstairs.

The upper landing was a straight hallway that was surprisingly wide. Three doors graced either side of the hallway for a total of six rooms on the upper floor. Ruth briefly thought it was a shame that so many bedrooms would be wasted on only two children in the household.

She continued to follow as Abigail chose one of the doors. It opened into a child's bedroom, containing two beds. Ruth was even more amazed to realize that both Abigail and Betty must share this room. After all, there were six bedrooms in the house in which such a small family lived. For what purposes were the other bedrooms used?

Ruth reviewed the room, taking in the plain wooden headboards of the small twin beds and the single heavy bureau that was so severe in its design that it stood like a monolith towering over the children. It was a barren room; without warmth or personality. The weak winter sun vainly attempted to shine through the single window, but the linen curtains were drawn, and only a thin stream of sunlight escaped through the part in the cloth.

The room was gloomy, and this added to Ruth's sense of uneasiness. She stood, feeling foolish, not knowing what to do now that she was actually inside the bedroom.

"What now?" Ruth finally asked.

"Take off your outerwear," Abigail instructed, "and lay it on Betty's bed."

"Why my bed?" Betty asked.

"Because we're going to sit on *my* bed, you silly goose," Abigail snapped.

"Why do you talk to Betty that way?" Ruth asked as she stripped her coat from her shoulders. "She's your cousin, after all."

"She's stupid," Abigail said in a matter of fact manner, as though it were so obvious that it shouldn't have been necessary to explain.

"Leave me alone," Betty pouted. "I'm not stupid."

"No, you're not stupid," Abigail suddenly smiled and spoke to Betty with surprising kindness. "You're my good little cousin."

Astonished at the sudden about-face, Ruth peered intently at Abigail, uncomprehending whatever she had just heard. Feeling confused, she decided to make no comment on the chameleon-like change in Abigail Williams. She carefully placed her coat on Betty's bed and then sat on the other. Betty sat next to her.

Abigail remained standing, facing her captive audience. "You know that Tituba Indian is from Barbados," she announced, "but do you know where that is?"

When neither Ruth nor Betty could answer, Abigail continued, "It's an island in the West Indies, and that's somewhere in the Caribbean Sea. But I'll bet you don't even know where the Caribbean Sea is. Well, let me tell you about Barbados. There are *witches* on that island, and Tituba is one of them!"

Ruth heard Betty gasp beside her. "No," Betty spoke, "Tituba is *not* a witch. She's really nice."

"What makes you say Tituba is a witch?" Ruth asked.

"She's a Negress, isn't she?" Abigail carefully put the egg she was holding on top of Betty's bed, and when she was sure it wouldn't roll, she took off her outerwear and laid it on top of the other coats.

"The Proctors have a Negro slave, and he's from Africa," Ruth said. "The Proctors' slave is certainly no warlock."

"Well," Abigail straightened up minus her outerwear, "I know that Tituba is a witch because she taught me some witchcraft."

Once again, Ruth heard an intake of breath from Betty. She moved to look at the young child, and realized that Betty was sitting straight and stiff, her face drained of color.

Abigail turned and retrieved the egg from the bed and held it up for the others to view. It was as though she wanted to make it clear that it was an ordinary egg. Seeming to enjoy her showmanship, Abigail said to Ruth, "This egg will show you when you are going to die. Tituba taught me some magic words to cast a witchcraft spell."

Ruth's mouth dropped open and she watched intently as Abigail went to the pitcher on top of the plain bureau and poured water into a glass. The dark-haired, small-eyed girl maneuvered the water pitcher with one hand while she continued to hold the egg with the other. She placed the glass of water on the bare wooden floor and then stood erect. Abigail spoke slowly, her voice soft yet menacing.

"Witches that fly, when will Ruth die?"

Ruth could feel Betty shift nervously on the bed and she glanced at the ten-year-old girl again. She could see that Betty was terrified. Ruth forced herself to turn around to see what Abigail was going to do next.

Abigail smiled her mirthless smile, the corners of her mouth upturned in almost a sneer. Dramatically she cracked the egg and let the contents spill into the glass of water where the white and the yolk began to sink to the bottom. The milky embryonic fluid that surrounded the golden orb drifted gracefully and blended with the water to create a filmy, semi-transparent swirl. The orange-yellow yolk hit the bottom of the glass and bounced, rising slightly from the bounce and then elongating into an odd form.

"The shape of the egg is changing," Abigail whispered as she squatted next to the glass on the floor. "It's showing us the future because I cast a spell. Now I can predict when you're going to die."

But then Abigail jerked her head up in surprise, because suddenly the bedroom door swung open.

Chapter Two

Startled, Ruth's pulse raced as she turned to see who was entering the room. Who was coming in to catch the girls performing unnatural acts?

Suddenly the meaning of what they were doing hit her, and Ruth was horrified. She experienced extreme fear that she would be caught and held accountable for the ungodly actions in which she was a participant. Her heart pounded in terror and sweat sprouted on her forehead.

It was a woman who walked through the bedroom door, a tall maidservant whose appearance was so striking that she would have commanded attention anywhere. The woman had coffee-with-cream skin, black eyes and high cheekbones, and instead of the typical black or gray somber clothing of the Villagers, this woman wore a colorfully woven scarf tied over her hair as though it were a turban. It would have been impossible to guess her age, because she could have been anywhere between twenty-five and forty-five. Although her house dress was the typical plain servant attire, the whole effect of the woman's appearance was one of exotic elegance.

"Tituba!" Betty cried, jumping from the bed into the woman's arms. "I'm so scared!"

"Wot be this?" said the heavily accented woman as she gathered Betty into her skirts. "Why you be fearful, little one?"

Then Tituba's look of surprise rapidly changed into a fierce scowl of consternation as she took in the scene before her. "Wot be happening here?" She shut the bedroom door and stepped inside. Betty let go of the skirt and stood alongside Tituba, making her alliance to the servantmaid clear.

Abigail quickly grabbed the glass that still contained the egg, and turned around so her back was turned to the servantmaid. Ruth watched in horror as Abigail put the glass to her lips and began to drink the contents. The raw mucus slid into Abigail's mouth and the egg disappeared.

"I asked a question," Tituba said stiffly, "and the answer is to be told."

Realizing that Abigail was unable to speak, Ruth said, "Abigail was showing me a game."

"No! No she wasn't!" Betty cried, still standing next to Tituba. She seemed so upset that her voice took a fevered pitch. "Abigail was casting a spell! A witchcraft spell!"

"Abigail," Tituba commanded, "turn around and let Tituba see wot is in the hand."

Abigail turned around, her face masked with indifference. "Just an empty glass. I was thirsty, so I drank a glass of water from the pitcher."

"Wot be wrong with Betty?"

"She fell asleep," Abigail said, "and she had a nightmare, that's all."

"I did not!" Betty practically wailed. "You told me that Tituba showed you how to make witch spells." Turning to Tituba, Betty said, "Abigail says you're a witch!"

"I be no witch and I no teach witchcraft," Tituba said firmly, "but you, Abigail Williams, you be a very wicked girl. You stop scaring your cousin or I be telling your uncle."

Abigail seemed to straighten her posture until she appeared somehow taller, somehow threatening in her stance. She spoke slowly and her voice held quiet malice. "You will do nothing of the sort. Because if you say anything to my uncle, I will get you. And I'll get you good."

Tituba gasped. "Wot you be meaning by that?"

"You'd just better not say anything, ever."

For a few moments it was a standoff...a showdown. Both Tituba and Abigail stood staring eye to eye without blinking, each taking a measure of the other. Then suddenly, to Ruth's surprise, Tituba lowered her gaze and took a step backwards.

Ruth wondered, *What have I just witnessed? A display of power by a twelve-year-old child over an adult?*

"Dinner be ready. Wash your hands and come downstairs, all of you." With that, the servantmaid gently pushed Betty out of her way and opened the bedroom door. Leaving the door ajar, Tituba vanished.

"You little snitch," Abigail hissed at Betty.

Betty stood trembling, pale and frightened.

"Leave her alone," Ruth said, rising from the bed upon which she had been sitting.

Abigail suddenly became bland and unconcerned "Let's rinse our hands in the basin and then go downstairs."

"Wait," Ruth said, "did you find out anything about me from the egg? Do you know when I'm supposed to die?"

"You're only seventeen," Abigail spoke flatly and without interest. "I imagine you'll have a few years left."

Ruth stood in surprise and watched as Abigail poured water from the pitcher and rinsed her hands in the basin. She wondered why Abigail was toying with her. What was her motive? Ruth wasn't so certain that she liked Abigail very much, but she couldn't deny that everything about Abigail was morbidly fascinating.

When the girls entered the hallway, Ruth turned to head back towards the servants' staircase, but Abigail stopped her by saying, "Not that one. Betty and I use the main staircase almost all the time. The servants' staircase is only to be used for secret things."

The main staircase made for a safer descent than had the servants' staircase for the ascent. The main staircase was wide and contained a banister and shallow steps. Ruth descended the stairs in second place; this time it was Betty who trailed behind.

Ruth entered the formal dining room, and took in the scene before her. She saw that all the guests were already seated. Her own father was sitting at the foot of the table, in the seating position normally reserved for the wife of the household. In the

Parris household, the wife was noticeably absent, but Ruth knew that Mrs. Parris was too sick to get out of bed.

Ruth's father was a tall man with wide shoulders. He had closely cropped graying hair and a well manicured gray beard. Her mother sat next to him; a thin woman who was also taller than most Puritan ladies. She wore her course, graying hair piled upon her head covered by a linen kerchief. Both Putnams would not put on their usual headgear until they left the dining room table and ventured back outside.

Ruth noticed that her two sisters, Hannah and Susanna, were also already seated. Out of ten siblings, only she and these two sisters remained in the Putnam household. Ruth was now the youngest child in the family, and most of the other Putnam siblings had already taken wives or taken residence in the houses of their husbands.

Ruth's brothers had homesteaded on portions of the Putnam farm, and the result was that now the farm was divided into smaller sections. The land upon which her brothers resided would become legally theirs once her father died. Ruth briefly remembered what Abigail had said earlier: "Your father told my uncle that unless you marry, he feels no obligation to give you any parcels of his land. Your father said that his land can only stretch so far, and he has fine sons who need to inherit. Maybe your family isn't as rich as you think they are!"

Oh no, Ruth wondered desperately, *can the things that Abigail told me about my father's farm really true? If so, then is it also true that I might have to live in the Parris household and become a servant to these people? Never! It can't be true!*

"Children, sit down," Reverend Parris instructed in his strong voice. He was seated at the head of the table, an appropriate display to demonstrate that Reverend Parris was indeed the head of the household. Ruth's attention turned to the minister as she sat next to Susanna, her sister. Ruth could understand how the Village congregation would be eager to hear God's Word out of this man, for he had a commanding presence that implied he was a leader of others. She noticed he wasn't exceptionally tall; still, he seemed larger than he was because he possessed an energy that made it appear he almost *willed* people into submission. He had a long nose, but his fierce brown eyes and strong chin made him almost handsome. A shock of thick brown hair tumbled down onto his wide forehead, giving him a rakish appearance.

When everyone was seated, Reverend Parris began, "Let us all pray and thank the good Lord for our bounty."

Ruth bowed her head and listened to the dinner sermon.

"Lord God," Parris began, "two families have come together in fellowship tonight. We give thanks for your generosity in providing this food for which we are about to eat. May your generosity and good will extend to us so that you will use Your power to block the attempts of Israel Porter to interfere with the congregation of Salem Village. We beseech you to smite Israel Porter down and to grant us the justice we so humbly deserve. Amen. You may all begin to eat."

Ruth was dumbstruck, and she numbly raised her head to make sure that the odd prayer was finished. She risked a glance at Reverend Parris out of the corner of her eye, and noticed that he appeared unconcerned that he had just asked God to smite someone down. What was going on? Who was Israel Porter?

Then Ruth became distracted because suddenly Tituba appeared and placed a huge steaming bowl of stew on the table. The servantmaid began ladling it into individual bowls. Tituba's husband John appeared with loaves of bread, which he also placed upon the table.

Ruth was hesitant as she reached for a portion of the bread. But then she recognized that the bread was made of ground wheat. Ruth had never liked the strong flavor of rye bread and so she was relieved that she would not have to eat it tonight.

The food was uniquely spiced, and very good. It was consumed as the elders talked. As was custom, the children deferred to the parents and by doing so, remained silent. But Ruth listened to the conversation between her father and the Reverend, trying to comprehend it all but understanding very little.

"The Villagers aren't paying their just contributions towards my salary," Reverend Parris was complaining to Ruth's father. "Even that beggarwoman, Sarah Good, must eat better than *my* family does. And here's another thing: I was promised that I would be provided with firewood. Now I have to pay for it out of my savings. Whoever deceives a man of God should be cursed."

"Maybe you should meet with the Village Council," Ruth heard her father advise.

"Council!" Parris blustered. "They can't be trusted. Well, this is beyond belief. Judas was given thirty pieces of silver to betray Jesus. Was that all Jesus was worth way back then? How much is Jesus worth now, to the people of Salem Village? They think hearing God's Word should be free? I need more money."

"Reverend," Mr. Putnam said, "we *all* need more money. That's why we can't afford to pay the exorbitant taxes that Israel Porter deems we must pay. Porter lives in Salem Village but represents Salem Town. What right does he have to take the hard earned money of the Salem Villagers?"

"Because he has the courts in his pockets," answered Parris. "Israel Porter can get away with it and he knows it. But let's get back to the point at hand. I need your help to convince the Villagers that I need more money. Nobody can expect me to survive on the inadequate amount of salary that I've been paid as of late."

"What am I supposed to do?"

"You can be a guest speaker at church this Sunday. You have influence over the Villagers and I'd like you to use it. It would be God's work, of course."

"Well," Mr. Putnam spoke slowly and thoughtfully, "I suppose I can do that. But Israel Porter has to be dealt with sooner or later. In the meantime, there are the situations of my three youngest daughters. Perhaps you can do something for me in return for my assistance to you."

Ruth was instantly alert, because she knew that whatever came next would decide the fate of her and her sisters. Still, she remained silent. As was her role, she was not to interrupt or interfere with the adults' conversations in any manner. She leaned forward in frightened anticipation. What were her father's intentions?

"I know of two men who are currently looking for wives," Parris answered, "and I am sure an arrangement can be made for two of your daughters to find marriage prospects. However, perhaps these two bachelors should be bequeathed to your oldest unmarried daughters. May I suggest that Ruth, being the youngest, has more time to find a suitable husband, so she should be the one to come into my household."

There! There it was, said out loud. Ruth's heart sank and she cringed in horror at the way her fate had been decided, without any considerations for her feelings.

But what was she to do? She understood her father's attempt to recruit the Village minister to help marry off his single daughters. To be a spinster would be a loathsome fate. She and her sisters would lose all respect in the community and would be treated as outcasts if they never married.

And yet there were only two suitable bachelors for three sisters, according to Reverend Parris. Ruth wondered, *Why, oh why isn't there a third eligible bachelor for me?*

It would be just as bad, if not even worse, if she were to become a servant. Was she to answer to the commands of others? How could her father submit her to such a fate? After all, she was a Putnam!

Her father continued speaking, "All of my three unmarried daughters have individual qualities that make them stand apart from the other girls in the Village. Any man in his right mind would feel lucky to marry any one of them. However, of all my daughters, I believe it is Ruth who is the most beautiful. So she would be desirable for a man just as much, if not more, than her older sisters would be."

"Vanity is a sin," Parris reminded Mr. Putnam, "and beauty is as beauty does. I'll tell you why Ruth should not be the daughter chosen to accept one of the bachelors. Your other daughters have all had more teaching as to how to be a wife because they both helped your neighbor, Doctor Griggs, when his wife was stricken ill and died. Hannah and Susanna took care of his children. By the time Ruth was old enough to help Doctor Griggs along with her sisters, he moved across the Village and was no longer available. So Ruth was never able to benefit from helping in Doctor Griggs's household."

Parris took a drink of water, then continued, "Ruth would be unmarketable for a husband unless she is suitably trained and ready to become a wife. That's why she needs to spend time in my household. Tituba can teach her how to cook and clean, and Ruth can care for Betty, which will teach her how to manage children. Also, I can put Ruth to work during church services to care for the Village infants. Ruth is at a disadvantage in your household, because she is the youngest. Therefore she has no younger siblings from which to acquire the child-rearing skills that are so necessary for a wife to know. But she can learn these skills by working for me."

Ruth glanced desperately around the table. The faces of her family were turned away from her. She tried to get her mother's attention, but Mrs. Putnam was also turned away, intently listening to the minister as he single-handedly decided Ruth's fate. Dejected and depressed, Ruth realized that she would receive no help from her mother.

Catching Abigail's eye, Ruth noticed that she was the only one looking in her direction. Abigail wore a satisfied smirk on her face.

So her fate was decided. Ruth understood that God commanded her to honor the wishes of her father, and therefore there was no way out. But her heart ached and her spirits sank.

And when the meal was over, the Putnam family left the Parris household.

Only Ruth remained behind.

That night, she cried herself to sleep. She muffled the sounds in her pillow, for she wanted no one to know that her heart was breaking. There would be no one in this household to comfort her. Instinctively she understood that the people in this household would only deem her weak if they knew she cried. Ruth knew she needed to keep up the illusion that she was strong, because she was getting the impression that some people in this household tended to prey upon the weak.

It was a night that seemed without end.

But it did end. The next morning, Ruth opened her eyes well before dawn. The room was dark and for a moment she thought she was home. Then reality hit her and she remembered. She was sleeping in the Parris house.

Her nose was cold, and Ruth snuggled deeper under her quilt. She knew that Reverend Parris kept his house cold because he continuously complained that firewood was expensive. Perhaps Reverend Parris felt that being a man of God was a noble calling, but he was obviously disenchanted with the salary it paid.

She was just starting to drift back to sleep when there was a loud knocking upon the bedroom door. "Get up!" called John Indian from the other side.

Startled, Ruth jerked in surprise. She sat up, the thick quilt tumbling off her shoulders, and the room's cold temperature slapped at her. Shivering, Ruth groped on the night table for the wooden matches. Her fingers probed the unfamiliar tabletop until she found them. Striking a match, the room suddenly became illuminated but the flickering flame created long shadows that danced upon the walls. She lit the oil lamp and still sitting up, looked at her surroundings.

She was in the bedroom next to the one in which Abigail and Betty slept. Her room was even barer than the children's bedroom, because it contained only one single bed. There was no furniture in this new room of hers except for the night table and an armoire. There was not even a chair upon which to sit.

Sighing, Ruth got out of the warm bed and braved the freezing room. She shed her heavy, scratchy nightdress and let it fall to the floor. Grabbing her dark brown woolen winter dress from out of the armoire, Ruth quickly pulled it over her head and let it fall into place. She belted her waist and straightened the wide, white collar and the cuffs at the sleeves.

She finished dressing with a white apron and a starched white cowl that she placed upon her head. It wouldn't do to ever be seen with her head uncovered, even this early in the morning. Sitting on the bed, she buttoned up her shoes.

Not sure how to start a day in the Parris household, Ruth was hesitant when she opened her bedroom door. Was she to go downstairs? What was the acceptable behavior in this house?

Standing in the hallway trying to decide, Ruth was again startled when suddenly Abigail and Betty's door burst open. The two girls tumbled out into the hallway, pushing each other and giggling, but they suddenly stopped short when they realized that Ruth was standing in front of them.

"Good morning," Ruth said lamely. The dim light from the hall candle created eerie shadows on the faces of the children as it flickered. She was aware of her own nervousness.

The other girls remained unmoving, silently staring at her. Then Betty timidly greeted her. "Hello," was all Betty said.

But Abigail was not so friendly. "Why are you just standing there?"

"I don't know what to do."

"Well, then, you're just as stupid as Betty," Abigail said.

"Quit calling me stupid!" Betty cried, and Ruth rolled her eyes, thinking that these two must squabble constantly.

Suddenly Ruth decided it was enough. "You're a very spiteful little girl," she told Abigail. "I don't know why you seem to dislike everybody."

"I may be spiteful, but I'm not little, and don't you forget it," Abigail snapped. "And I only dislike people who deserve to be disliked."

Ruth raised her eyebrows. "So, are you saying that I deserve to be disliked?"

Abigail stared for a moment, appraising Ruth. Then she said, "I don't know yet. I'm still deciding what to think about you, so you'd better be nice to me."

Suddenly, Abigail once again became the chameleon, because abruptly she brightened and said, "Betty and I will show you what to do. First we need to go downstairs for family prayer and a Bible study. Then we'll have breakfast. Come along with us."

Would Ruth ever understand this child? It seemed that Abigail was temperamental, almost unstable. Did Reverend Parris keep her suitably chastised? If so, did Abigail only show this side of herself to people who were not in a position of authority over her?

Ruth had an uneasy feeling, and she knew that she would not be trusting Abigail Williams any time in the near future. She understood that to ever let Abigail know she was afraid to be here would leave her vulnerable to psychological attacks. She vowed silently to herself that she would always remain on guard any time that Abigail was in her presence.

Always in the lead, Abigail preceded the small group of girls back to the main staircase. The three girls clattered down the stairs, and when they reached the bottom, Ruth noticed that just now, John Indian was lighting the parlor fire. She was flabbergasted to realize that the Parris household had been without a fire the entire night. No wonder it was so cold in this house!

Reverend Parris suddenly strode into the parlor, his posture firm and his demeanor stern. "All of you, get into the dining room. We're late for our prayer meeting at the main table."

Late? Ruth wondered. *It's an hour away from dawn yet. At what time does this family usually arise?*

The girls took seats at the dining room table, where Tituba Indian was already seated. Having finished with the parlor fire, Tituba's husband John joined everyone. Ruth was pleased to see that the servants were included in the prayer meeting. Perhaps it was a sign that Reverend Parris was kind to his workers.

Parris again took his place at the head of the table. If Ruth had thought him kind to his servants, she was mistaken, for he announced, "Ruth, I allow the Indians to attend my prayer meetings because they are from a heathen land, and servants are better behaved if they understand and obey the Word of God. After all, in Malachi, the Bible says, *A servant honoreth his master.* My servants need to obey me, for in this house, I am the master."

Ruth remained silent. But she understood that the Reverend felt his servants were to be treated no better than a horse or an ox; possessions that were simply there to serve a master.

"We will begin with Psalm Seventy-Four," Reverend Parris said, then began to quote the Bible. "Arise, oh God, plead thine own cause: remember how a foolish man reproacheth thee daily. Forget not the voice of thine enemies, as the tumult of those that rise up against thee increaseth continually."

What does that mean? Ruth wondered.

Reverend Parris put down the Bible and said, "Just as it was in the times when the Bible was written, there are enemies among our midst in these current times today. We must study the Bible so that we may be armed with the knowledge about how to fight our enemies. The Bible will show us how to proceed."

Uneasy, Ruth kept her eyes lowered. Where were the scriptures about loving thy neighbors? All her life, Ruth had been taught that the Lord was a loving God, a merciful God. But Parris seemed intent to seek out the darkest passages in what should have been a Good Book.

Because she was deep within her own thoughts, Ruth missed most of the rest of the Bible study. She paid no attention to anything more that Reverend Parris said, because it all seemed to be within the same theme, and jumbled together.

She glanced at the others, and noticed that both Abigail and Betty were vacantly staring at the table in front of them, as though they had heard all this before. Tituba appeared to have her thoughts elsewhere. John had his eyes closed, and for all she could tell, he might have been sleeping.

The study droned on and on, and Ruth continued to drift in her thoughts, not hearing any of it. Finally, Reverend Parris said something that Ruth did not catch as he closed the Bible with a *snap*.

Coming out of her musings, Ruth noticed that it was suddenly silent in the room and everybody was staring at her. Even John Indian was now awake, staring at her.

"What?" Ruth asked, embarrassed.

"I said you will come to the church with me this morning." Parris was obviously repeating a prior statement he had made.

Ruth said, "But why? Today is Saturday."

His face dark, Parris said, "Because you will need to be shown around the children's room at the church. You start your duties there tomorrow. An efficient person is a prepared person. As soon as the first rays of the sun come up, we'll be on our way. But in the meantime, my wife is, as you know, an invalid. Your job in this household will be to care for my wife. She will need her bedpan now, so get to it."

Ruth sat very still for a moment, then said, "I thought my duties were to learn to keep house and to watch Betty so I could learn about being a wife myself and about having children."

"Don't be insolent!" Reverend Parris thundered. "Your duties in this house are to be whatever I say they are! And right now, you are to attend to my wife! So get out of this room and do it."

Suddenly Parris stood, and towered over Ruth. Then he added, "It says in Saint Luke, *Blessed be the servant*. You, Ruth, are blessed because you are now a servant in the house of a man of God."

Ruth felt as though she could not catch her breath. Instantly she understood that she was in the same position as were Tituba and John Indian. She realized that she was to be treated as a horse or an ox; as a possession. She was a servant who was to obey the every whim of Reverend Samuel Parris.

Chapter Three

They walked to the church.

It was cold, and Ruth listened to her feet crunch on the snow, because they walked without speaking. She walked to the right and slightly behind Reverend Parris as was custom. She had her winter outerwear pulled tightly across her shoulders as protection against the February cold, and she had a woolen scarf draped across the lower portion of her face. Her nose was free of the scarf and she watched the little puffs of mist blow out with every exhalation, her breath visible in the cold winter air.

She was glad that Parris lived so close to the church and soon she could see the building ahead of them. It appeared much smaller than the house where she was staying. Unlike the Parris house, the church was the color of the wood from which it was built; however, the outer walls had been heavily oiled as protection against the elements. It was a simple one-story building, with a room obviously added onto the back.

They entered the threshold of the church, stamping their feet to be rid of the snow clinging to their boots. Ruth looked around the familiar place; she had been attending church all her life. She thought about how the church had changed over the years.

Ruth knew that there had been a lot of controversy between Salem Village and Deodat Lawson, the minister who was employed here prior to Reverend Parris. She remembered that at the time, a lot of Villagers had not felt that Lawson was an appropriate choice to minister to the congregation. But she had been too young to understand specifically what the controversy had been about. Still, she knew that eventually the congregation had determined that Lawson was not the right minister to spread

God's Word to Salem Village, and had driven him out.

Now, as she looked at Samuel Parris, Ruth wondered to herself, *Is this minister any better for Salem Village than was the last?*

Instantly Ruth felt tremendous guilt for her silent question and she fervently hoped that the Lord God had been distracted for just that one moment and hadn't known her thoughts.

"Take off your winter gear," Parris instructed. Sighing, Ruth removed and hung up her outerwear on one of three racks placed by the inside door. She noticed that Parris left his outerwear on, but she was afraid to ask him any questions.

"Follow me," Reverend Parris commanded, and Ruth trailed behind him. Parris led her down the center isle of the church between the crudely carved wooden pews. She followed the minister up to the front of the church where Parris suddenly stopped and stared at the area which contained the pulpit.

"Someday this church will be grander," Ruth heard Parris say quietly. "I cannot preach effectively unless I have grander surroundings."

Then he turned and looked at her. "Your role in this church from now on will be to watch the children who are too young to attend my services. I won't have my preaching disrupted by crying infants. You will keep them quiet or else you will risk my wrath."

Ruth nodded, then once again followed Parris as he led her into the back room.

"Here," he said, "this is where you will be working tomorrow. Stay here now and make the room ready for Sunday's children. I'll be back in about an hour to get you. Clean this place up! You have enough to do here to keep you busy for an hour. But be warned, if this room is not absolutely spotless when I return, you will be punished."

With that, Reverend Parris turned on his heels. He slammed the door that divided the church and the back room. Ruth could hear him stomping down the center aisle, then she heard the front door also slam.

He is so pent up with anger, Ruth thought with surprise.

She looked around the room. It was indeed a mess, with wooden toys strewn about and stools overturned. She sighed again and began the task of straightening and cleaning.

About fifteen minutes into her task, she heard the front door of the church open again. Was Reverend Parris back so soon? Panicked, Ruth realized that she had barely put a dent into cleaning the back room. He needed to at least give her a chance to do what she had been told!

Frozen, Ruth listened to footsteps approach. Then she heard an unfamiliar voice. It sounded like that of a man much younger than Parris.

"Who's here?" the young man's voice called.

Ruth hesitated, unsure of whether or not to respond.

"I know someone is in here, because there's a coat hanging," the voice called again. "Who's here?"

She jerked herself out of inaction and went to the door of the back room. Slowly Ruth opened the door, and put her head through it to see into the main room of the church. "I'm here," she said timidly.

When he saw her, the young man's face brightened.

"And who might you be?" he asked as he strode in her direction. He was about twenty or twenty-one, with light brown hair, tall and lean. As he got closer, Ruth noticed two things: one, that the color of his eyes matched the color of his hair, and two, that he was exceedingly handsome.

Handsome or not, he was a stranger. Ruth stepped backwards into the children's room, but left the dividing door open. "I'll not tell you who I am unless I know who you are first," she told the young man.

He continued to smile, and his eyes twinkled in amusement. He stepped into the back room and began to take off his outerwear. Tossing his coat onto a stool, the man explained, "I'm William. I've come here to find the Reverend. I've been by his house, and they told me he was here. Obviously he's *not* here. But you are, and I think that's an even better find."

ACCUSED: A TALE OF THE SALEM WITCH TRIALS

What a rascal, Ruth thought. Out loud she introduced herself. "I'm Ruth Putnam, and I'm staying with the Parris family for a while."

Outwardly solemn, William kissed her hand, but his eyes still held the amusement as before. "Well, you certainly must beautify that household. You are very pretty, do you know that?"

Disdainfully, Ruth wrinkled her nose, and quoted what she had heard Reverend Parris say just the night before. "Vanity is a sin," she told William, "and beauty is as beauty does."

To her surprise, William began to laugh uproariously. Offended, Ruth asked angrily, "What? What is so funny?"

Quieting down but still grinning, William responded, "I see you've already been influenced by Reverend Parris. Well, maybe there's a few things you should know about the 'fine and upstanding' minister of Salem Village."

Detecting the sarcasm in his voice, Ruth found herself intrigued. Would this stranger be able to supply her with some of the answers to her questions about Reverend Parris? Or would whatever he had to tell her be simply gossip, just hearsay, not to be taken with any grains of truth?

She decided it would be the latter. "I have work to do," she said. "I need to clean up this room. I don't have time to listen to your stories. Besides, what did you want with Reverend Parris?"

"I need to talk to him about business," William answered. Then, to her surprise, he began picking up toys off the floor. "I'll help you clean."

"No, that's not necessary!" Ruth exclaimed, pulling a toy out of William's hand. "Cleaning is women's work."

Again he laughed. "It's a small price for me to pay if I can talk to you. After all, you did say you didn't have time to listen to my stories, didn't you? Well, if I were to help you in here, then you'd have the time, wouldn't you? That way, we'd both be happy, as you need to clean and I need to talk."

Exasperated, Ruth handed William back the toy she had taken out of his hands. "This is most unusual," was all she could think to say.

"I'm an unusual kind of guy," he smiled.

"We need to keep the door to this room wide open, or else it wouldn't be proper for you to be alone in here with me," she reminded him.

"That's fine," he answered, and walking to the door, made an exaggerated show of opening it as wide as the hinges would allow.

Charmed by this man, Ruth allowed him into the back room with her. Secretly she was glad for his company, because she decided that she liked him very much. They worked side by side for a few minutes, neither of them speaking.

Finally Ruth asked, "Well, you said you had stories to tell and so far I haven't heard a word out of you. What do you know about Reverend Parris?"

Not stopping the cleaning, William began, "You know that he's been the minister of Salem Village since 1689. But it was a really close decision whether or not to hire Samuel Parris, because a lot of the Villagers didn't trust him."

Pausing, he looked at her. "Isn't your father John Putnam?"

When she nodded, William continued, "Well, your father was paramount in the decision to hire Samuel Parris. Your father does favors for Parris."

Indignant, Ruth exclaimed, "You're lying!"

"No, no, just hear me out. I never said your father wasn't a good man, because he is. But your father doesn't like Israel Porter. There's a huge feud between the Putnam and the Porter families. Your father just needs Parris' assistance on political matters sometimes where the Porters are concerned. It's no big deal."

Calmed, Ruth said, "Tell me more about Reverend Parris. He seems frequently angry. Do you know why?"

"Because the good Reverend can't seem to figure out where he belongs in life," William answered. "For one thing, he's bitter because he didn't get an inheritance from his father. Then he tried going to college but I hear he didn't finish. Maybe he just wasn't motivated enough to finish his higher education. But some people say that Parris constantly lost his temper and argued with his professors, and these same people say that eventually Parris was forced to leave college because once he had come to blows with an instructor."

William put the crudely carved wooden toys he had collected into a big box in the corner, then began straightening the sitting stools until they were all upright. "After college, Parris became a businessman, but not a very good one. You see, Ruth, he kept going from one unsuccessful business venture to another, and all of them failed."

William continued, "He lived in Boston before he came here, and when each of his business venture attempts went under, he eventually became penniless. In fact, he found himself deeply in debt. Maybe this explains why Parris feels such an intense need for money nowadays."

Fascinated, Ruth found herself staring at William. "What happened next?"

"Parris was hired as a foreman on the Boston jury of Appellants and Appeals, where he just so happened to hear a case by your father. That's how he got to know your father."

Ruth found herself bristling again, and she practically threw a sewn cloth doll into the corner toy box. "My father wouldn't have any reason to be in Boston. And even if he did, you're making it sound as though he struck a deal with Reverend Parris."

Still smiling, William continued, "Lots of court cases wind up in Boston. I never said that your father isn't a good man, because he *is* a good man. But that particular court case had to do with the rights to a waterway. I don't know if you know this, but your father shares a river with Israel Porter, and sometimes there are disputes over a dam built upon it. That's one of the reasons for the feud. Believe me, the feud between the Putnams and the Porters has gone back for generations."

"What happened next?" Ruth repeated.

"After his duties to the Appellant Court were finished," William told her, "Parris became ordained as a minister. He applied for the position here in Salem Village and your father petitioned to hire him. Israel Porter petitioned against hiring Parris. Eventually your father prevailed, because here Parris is."

"I heard that Israel Porter collects taxes for the Town," Ruth commented, "even though he lives here in the Village."

"And so he does," William said. "That's yet another reason for the feud. Your father is one of the richest farmers in the Village. So he has to pay the most taxes."

Ruth looked around the room, which seemed perfectly clean at that point. She sat on one of the stools. "Why doesn't Israel Porter have to pay the same amount of taxes as does my father? His land is in the Village, too."

"Because Porter is on the Town committee," William answered. "Israel Porter works as an intermediary between Salem Town and Salem Village. He helps settle disputes between the two. He also ensures that Town aid is to be provided for the Village. More importantly, Porter arranges the sales of Village crops to the townfolk. It all works out. Although Reverend Parris dislikes Israel Porter intensely, he realizes that Porter is vital to the continuing health of the Village community. Like I said, it all works out."

Suddenly Ruth heard the front door of the church slam, and she realized that the Reverend must have returned. William picked up his coat, then quickly grabbed her hand and kissed it.

"I'll see you again," he grinned at her, "and trust me, you can believe that I'll see you again very soon."

She felt her face flush as her heart raced. William turned and went to the main room of the church to greet the Reverend. Ruth remained behind in the back room, where she looked quickly around and saw that it seemed perfectly clean. So she sat on a stool in the corner and strained to try to listen to the conversation between Parris and the young man she liked very, very much.

Despite her attempts, she realized that she could hear none of the conversation taking place in the other room. Frustrated, she knew she had to simply be patient and wait by herself in the back room. She settled down because she thought that the two men might take awhile to finish whatever business they had to discuss together.

But after only a few moments, Ruth heard Parris yell, "Get out of here!"

Surprised and a bit frightened, Ruth stiffened. She remained sitting on her stool until Reverend Parris came back into the children's room. Noticing his face was red and his eyes blazing, Ruth cringed, not knowing what sort of behavior to expect out of such a volatile man.

He didn't even appear to notice that the children's room was now neat and clean. "Get up and get your coat on," he roared at her, "because we're going back home!"

"Where's William?" Ruth asked.

"I threw him out," Parris said, then stopped and examined her closely. "Were you talking to him?"

Unsure how to answer, Ruth stumbled on her words. "I . . .well . . .he did speak to me, but not very much."

"You are forbidden to ever talk to him again!" Parris bellowed. "Don't you know who that heathen is?"

"No. I only know that his name is William."

"He's a Porter!" Parris continued to yell.

"He's a Porter?" she repeated numbly.

"He's Israel Porter's son."

Ruth's heart sank at the news, because she realized that she had been looking forward to seeing William again.

But she understood that his being a Porter meant she would never be allowed to do so. The disappointment was almost overwhelming.

"Get your coat on," Parris commanded, "because you have work to do back at home. In fact, you'll have so much work that you won't have time to think about any of the Porters. Your father gave us grain last night, both wheat and rye. Unfortunately, some of the rye grain looks tainted, so we'll need to use it up right away before the whole lot goes bad. Today Tituba will show you how to bake bread."

Nodding, Ruth trailed after Reverend Parris as they walked back together. During the walk through the snow, Ruth's thoughts kept returning to William Porter. Why oh why did he have to be a Porter? He had been so handsome, so charismatic, so flirtatious. She liked him; even now her face flushed when she thought of him.

In her mind, Ruth knew she would never see William again. But in her heart, she wished she could.

When they reached the house, Parris instructed Ruth to join Tituba, who had already begun the baking process. He then turned around and left her on the stoop by herself, saying he had more errands to run. Ruth was secretly glad to be rid of him, if only for awhile.

She entered the house and removed her outerwear. She went into the kitchen, where Tituba was bustling inside. Tituba motioned for Ruth to join her.

Ruth watched Tituba add the ground rye flour to the mixture in the huge bowl. The Indian told her that the plan was to bake five loaves all at once, and so it seemed there was a very large quantity of dough. As Tituba ran her fingers to knead the mixture, Ruth wondered why the dough appeared to be such an odd color.

"Why does it look sort of reddish?" Ruth asked. "Is the rye mixture always that color?"

"Most times it be brown," Tituba explained with her heavy accent, "but this rye, it had some big kernels. Different rye makes different colors."

Ruth felt some doubt. "The Reverend told me that some of this rye grain is tainted. That's why he wanted us to use up the rye before the wheat."

"I be baking bread all my life, and all be good bread," Tituba smiled, then added, "Now, this bread needs to sit and rise. You go outside. The other girls be out back."

Glad for the respite, Ruth went upstairs once again to retrieve her winter outerwear. When she was sufficiently bundled, she passed through the kitchen and then went outside through the heavy wooden back door.

She could see Abigail and Betty in a corner by the barn. The two children were hunched over, staring intently at something in the snow. Curious, Ruth ventured to where the other girls were poised, unmoving.

"What are you looking at?" Ruth asked when she got within earshot.

"Come and see for yourself," Abigail answered, and pointed to the ground.

A circle of snow was red with blood. In the center of the stain was a dead rabbit, its entrails lying exposed. The rabbit appeared as though it had been killed by a dog, because its fur was ripped and torn.

"I wonder why the dog didn't eat it," Abigail said.

"This is disgusting," Ruth blurted. "Why are you both staring at it?"

"Because the guts tell the future by how they lay," Abigail met Ruth's eyes with her own small dark ones.

"Oh sure," Ruth spoke sarcastically, "just like you told me that an egg can show me when I'm going to die. Just like you told me that Tituba is a witch."

"She *is* a witch," Abigail continued to stare directly at Ruth, "but it's a secret. Tituba would never tell either one of you. You see, Tituba tells only me. What you'd consider to be bad might not be something that I'd consider to be bad. "

"Don't listen to her," Betty said, "because she's lying. Tituba is *not* a witch."

"Maybe I'm lying and maybe I'm not," Abigail's gaze returned to the lacerated animal. "Maybe Tituba teaches me witchcraft and maybe she doesn't. But you're not sure, are you? Anyway, do you want to know what I've learned about the future from looking at this dead rabbit or not?"

Ruth had to force herself to again look at the chewed and mutilated animal. It was not merely the idea that in front of her lay a dead rabbit; it was the idea that just a few hours ago, this had been a living and breathing animal. It was a demonstration that mortality was a very real concept. It was proof that a living being could suddenly cease to be. This rabbit was no longer able to think, to feel, to experience life. It was a reminder of the irrevocable fate that would eventually claim every living being.

Studying the rabbit, Ruth was mesmerized by the grim nature of death. It was such a mystery; there were so many questions that would never receive answers. Was there really a God in Heaven to receive one's souls? The rabbit looked so ultimate, so *final*. Was there really another life after death?

Ruth suddenly realized where her thoughts were leading, and she was shocked at herself for all the questions that were bordering upon heresy. But there were so many new things she couldn't seem to comprehend within the last few days. She was starting to question almost everything she was experiencing.

Despite her conviction that it was all some weird game Abigail was playing, Ruth found herself morbidly curious. "Okay," she ventured, "what does the rabbit's entrails show you?"

"See that?" Abigail pointed. "Look at the way the intestines are crossed over themselves. That means that someone here is about to do something evil."

"What do you mean?" Betty asked, once again appearing shaken and pale.

Abigail turned towards Betty to further frighten the younger girl. She narrowed her small dark eyes and spoke slowly, "What evil things are you doing?"

Betty took a step backwards and started to cry. "None, I swear!"

Ruth once again had had enough. "Now look what you've done. Stop torturing Betty. Leave her alone. She's just a kid."

"It's not Betty anyway who's about to do something evil," Abigail now turned back to Ruth, "it's you."

Ruth was getting angry. "Or maybe it's you."

Abigail shrugged. "Maybe it *is* me."

"Well, this is nonsense anyway. Where do you get all these witchcraft ideas?"

"I told you. Tituba is a witch. You'd better listen to me."

Suddenly someone called to the girls. Momentarily confused,

Ruth turned to look at the house, but no one was calling from there. She turned back around and saw that Abigail and Betty were looking in a different direction, and that Betty's tears had stopped.

Ruth turned her gaze in the other direction, and saw a middle-aged woman approaching though the snow, walking from the direction of the street. The woman was holding the hand of a young child, and practically dragging the little girl behind her.

"Who's that?" asked Ruth.

Abigail turned to Ruth. "Don't you know anything about Salem Village?"

"Not much," Ruth admitted. "My parents never let me go out very often and they never talked about anyone or anything besides my own family. Seems the only time I ever got out of the house was on Sundays when I went to church."

Abigail stared at Ruth for a moment, then explained, "That's Goody Good. Her full name is Sarah Good. She's just a beggar."

"Who's the little girl with her?"

"That's her daughter Dorcas," Betty jumped in before Abigail had a chance to reply. "Dorcas is four."

"Wow," Ruth mused as she waited for the beggarwoman to approach, "Goody Good looks almost too old to have a four-year-old child."

"She's a beggarwoman," Abigail repeated. "She looks old because she eats garbage and sleeps on the streets. God doesn't like people who beg, and neither do I."

"God doesn't like people who do witchcraft either," Ruth said.

"Witchcraft doesn't involve God," Abigail answered, and Ruth felt a chill that had nothing to do with the weather.

The woman reached the trio of girls, and Ruth saw that Goody Good actually had a pipe in her mouth. Her skin was weathered and lined from the elements, and her hair was uncombed and pigmented with iron gray streaks. Her clothes were well worn, and her pipe emitted an awful stench.

The small little girl was not faring any better. Her hair was also uncombed and her face was dirty. Dorcas wore oversized clothes that hung loosely on her small frame.

"What could good Christians such as yourself spare for the less fortunate?" The woman had spittle that gathered at the corners of her mouth when she spoke. She touched the dead rabbit with the toe of her shoe. "Hope you have something better to offer than this here dead rabbit."

"Goody Good," Abigail spoke loudly and with distaste, "get out of here. You stink."

"My, my, my, Abigail Williams! You think you're so high-and-mighty?" Sarah Good began to yell at Abigail. "You are just a beggar yourself! You have to beg your roof and your meals from your uncle! Why, you have no more a family of your own than I do."

Ruth felt fear course through her veins. She knew it made no sense, but suddenly she was absolutely certain that something harmful was going to happen to the beggarwoman because she had spoken to Abigail in such a manner.

It was an illogical fear, since after all, Abigail was only a twelve-year-old child. Nonetheless, Ruth felt in her heart that Abigail was a very dangerous person. How Abigail could be dangerous, Ruth had no idea, yet she was certain it was true.

Abigail narrowed her small dark eyes and took a step towards Sarah Good. Instinctively little Dorcas whimpered and hid behind her mother. Abigail drew herself upright until she stood straight and tall. She met the beggarwoman's eyes with her own, and began to speak with a voice that dripped with venom.

"You will live to regret this," Abigail said slowly.

"Oh is that so?" scoffed Sarah Good.

"Get off my uncle's property," Abigail said.

In desperation, Ruth stepped in front of Abigail. "Goody Good, you'd better go somewhere else now. I think you'd better leave Abigail alone."

Misinterpreting Ruth's intentions, Sarah Good began to yell again, "I am a freewoman, not a slave to be ordered around by children!"

"Please leave while you can," Ruth pleaded.

"You'll regret this," Abigail still glared at Sarah Good, "because I'll get you."

The beggarwoman hesitated. She seemed uncertain and no longer blustered. Finally, without a word, Sarah Good turned on her heels, and grabbing her young daughter's hand, she pulled the child behind her once again as she left. She huffed and the smoke trailed from the smelly pipe in her mouth as she stomped away.

Ruth felt sick in the pit of her stomach. She felt exhausted and her nerves were jangling. She had witnessed Abigail threaten two people over the two days she had been in the Parris household, Tituba yesterday, and now Goody Good today. So far nothing bad had happened to either Tituba or to the beggarwoman.

Yet Ruth felt certain that Abigail wouldn't let either of them go without punishment.

But how could Abigail accomplish it?

Shuddering, Ruth knew that she must be even more careful to always remain on guard whenever she was around Abigail Williams.

Later that day, at the table, Ruth bowed her head for grace, but didn't hear a word of it. It was not the inspiration she craved from the Bible. She decided to ignore most of Reverend Parris' sermons, for they were always bitter and full of malice. Ruth determined that she would from here on read the Bible on her own, alone in her room.

Upon the completion of the prayer, Tituba rose from the table to retrieve bread from the kitchen. When it was placed upon the table, Ruth could see that the bread was one of the rye loaves that she had helped Tituba bake.

"Bring a loaf of wheat!" Parris shouted. "Rye bread is for children and poor people. I am the master of this household, and you'd better respect that fact. Do I look like a child or a poor person? I don't eat rye!"

Tituba jumped so quickly to obey the command that a chair

tumbled backwards and fell upon the dining room floor with a loud *bang*. Tituba righted the chair, then fled into the kitchen to retrieve a loaf of wheat bread.

Ruth looked at the dark loaf of rye that had been left behind, still sitting in the center of the table. She decided that she didn't want to eat any of it, either. The strong flavor of rye had never suited her taste. She watched as little Betty Parris reached for a slice of the freshly baked rye bread.

Chapter Four

That night, there was a disturbance in the Parris household.

At around midnight, Ruth was awakened by sounds of crying originating from the bedroom next to hers. She was deeply buried into her quilts, and she had been dreaming, so it seemed she had to swim through layers of sleep to reach consciousness. But eventually the noise did waken her, and Ruth opened her eyes, seeing nothing because of the darkness of her room.

She lay in her bed, immobile, trying to make sense out of what she was hearing. One of the girls in the bedroom next door was sobbing, and Ruth listened carefully to determine which one.

It sounded like Betty.

Ruth continued to lie in bed without moving.

What should I do? she wondered. *Should I get up and see what's wrong?*

But she decided that she didn't need to do anything because Ruth heard the sounds of Reverend Parris coming down the hall. She listened as he opened the door to the room where Abigail and Betty slept.

Feeling like an eavesdropper, Ruth strained to hear. She knew that being nosy was devil's work, but she was so curious, she couldn't stop herself. She was eavesdropping simply because she wanted to know what was going on in the bedroom next door.

So she listened.

The sobbing sounds continued. She could hear Reverend Parris say, "What's going on in here? What's wrong with Betty?"

Try as she might, Ruth was unable to hear Abigail's response.

But then she heard the Reverend exclaim, "Look at her! She's in an unnatural position! I'll send John Indian to fetch Doctor Griggs."

She heard Parris leave the room and he clattered down the hallway. A few minutes later, she could hear him waking John and Tituba. Barking commands at John to go get the doctor, Parris then told Tituba to get dressed so she could go and be a nurse to Betty.

"Wake up Ruth and tell her to assist you!" Ruth could hear Parris scream at Tituba. There was a great deal activity following his commands, and within minutes, Ruth heard frantic knocking upon her bedroom door.

The door flung open, and Ruth was startled, so she jerked herself into a rigid upright position on the bed. "Who's there?" she cried because the light was behind the figure at the door. Ruth was not certain whether the person entering her room was Tituba or Reverend Parris.

But she relaxed when she heard Tituba's heavily accented voice say, "It be me. Hurry child, and get your clothes on. You be needed to help with Mistress Betty."

Tituba left and once again the room was enveloped in darkness. Ruth groped for the oil lamp and lit it. She threw off her quilts and rushed to put on her day clothes.

When she was dressed, Ruth went into the hallway and entered the room that housed Betty and Abigail. Standing in the doorway, Ruth stopped in surprise because her senses were overwhelmed by the scene inside the children's bedroom.

Abigail was seated on her own bed, staring at Betty. Tituba was sitting on the foot of Betty's bed, appearing helpless to intervene in the situation that was unfolding right in front of her.

Something was wrong with Betty. Something was very, very wrong.

Ruth gasped in alarm as she stood, her feet glued to the floor. She could feel her own eyes grow large within her face. Of all the aberrations she had endured in this household, Ruth felt that this was certainly the worst to witness.

Betty's behavior was abnormal, even deviant. The small

child's skin was a pale, sickly color resembling the underside of a fish belly. Like a fish, Betty flopped upon the bed in convulsions, and her head was turned around at an unnatural angle. Her tongue was extended out of her mouth at an impossible length, and although her sobbing had ceased, Betty was moaning, over and over, something that sounded like a guttural "Uhh, uhh, uhh."

Ruth threw her hands to her face, still standing in the doorway, immobile from shock. Never had Ruth ever imagined a human being could contort in such a hideous fashion. It didn't seem physically possible, yet it was happening right in front of her.

She forced herself into movement, and rushed to Betty's bed. Sitting and leaning forward, Ruth tried to take the child into her own arms to possibly soothe her, but Betty continued to flail around in jerking motions, slipping out of her grasp. She then tried to pin Betty down upon the bed to try to prevent her from writhing, but the child had unnatural strength, rendering Ruth ineffective in her efforts. Finally Ruth was reduced to whispering soothing sounds, and murmured "Shhh, it will be all right."

But nothing was all right. For about ten more minutes, Betty continued to convulse, and her tongue and neck stretched to unbelievable proportions.

Then suddenly it was all over, and Betty fell back upon the bed, sinking into the mattress and making a sighing sound. Her face remained pasty white, and her tongue still protruded, resting between open lips. Betty appeared to be unconscious, but at least she was finally still.

"Betty?" Ruth probed, but the child did not acknowledge her spoken name in any manner.

"Wot be wrong with the child?" Tituba asked.

"I don't know," Ruth answered. "I've never seen anything like this."

Suddenly Abigail spoke, still sitting on her bed. Ruth turned to look at her and was stunned by the malevolence of her expression.

"It's your fault, Tituba," Abigail hissed at the servantmaid. "You put a witchcraft spell on Betty."

Tituba sat back a bit at the foot of Betty's bed. "Wot you be saying to Tituba?"

Abigail mocked Tituba's accent. "I be saying you be a witch."

"Stop it!" Ruth exclaimed. "The things you're saying are ludicrous!"

"Oh are they?" Abigail now turned to glare at Ruth, her expression full of malice. "You said yourself that you've never seen anything like this before. You saw how Betty acted. She acted bewitched. You've got a better explanation?"

"I said stop it," Ruth repeated.

"I love Mistress Betty like she be my own child," Tituba said.

"You don't have to defend yourself," Ruth told the servantmaid. "Abigail is just upset. She doesn't mean anything she says."

Abigail turned to face Tituba, and accused, "You should have been a lot nicer to me. I know you love Betty. Like your own child, you just said. You always take her side on things. You never loved *me*, in fact, I don't think you ever even *liked* me. You really should have been a lot nicer to me."

"You be a wicked little girl," Tituba said.

"Tituba," Ruth warned, "now is not the time."

Abigail sat back upon her pillows. All three sat in silence for awhile, each keeping a quiet vigil over Betty, who remained unconscious.

After what seemed to be a long time, Reverend Parris came through the door, followed by Doctor Griggs. The Doctor didn't waste time with questions, but instead went directly to Betty's bedside to evaluate her for himself.

John Indian trailed in the rear, then stood against the wall of the bedroom, watching the scene in front of him. Tituba rose from Betty's bed and went to join her husband against the wall.

But Ruth watched in surprise as John moved a few feet away from his wife and told her, "You be a sinner, woman."

ACCUSED: A TALE OF THE SALEM WITCH TRIALS

Was there any end to the continuous bombardment of shocking things in this house? Ruth looked around but realized that no one had noticed the odd interaction between John and Tituba, because everyone still seemed to be concentrating on Betty and her mysterious condition.

Ruth had to stop for a moment and wonder, *Why would John call his wife a sinner? Oh no, does he think she's a witch too?*

But then the commotion at Betty's bed captured Ruth's attention once again. Another seizure gripped the little girl, and her back arched and her arms flailed. Betty's head turned to the left, and once again her tongue protruded out of her mouth.

"Get me a depressor to prop her mouth open or she'll bite off her tongue!" cried Doctor Griggs, "Get it out of my bag!"

Parris himself raced to fetch the instrument, and handed the flat wooden stick to Griggs. The Doctor shoved it in Betty's mouth, his body leaning upon the child's in an attempt to hold her still. For what seemed to be an endless amount of time, the Doctor struggled to keep Betty from hurting herself during her wild displays of frenzied movements.

Finally Betty's latest seizure ended, and she once again slipped into unconsciousness. Doctor Griggs continued to hold her down with his arms, but after a few minutes passed and Betty still did not move, he released his grip and sat down on her bed.

Grim faced, Reverend Parris asked what everyone wanted to know. "What's wrong with Betty?"

Doctor Griggs shook his head. "I'll bleed her. That should release any impurities from her system by getting rid of bad blood."

"But you must have some idea of the cause," Parris persisted as he sat on the bed next to the Doctor.

"It is caused by a bad miasma. Let me bleed her, and then we'll see."

Everyone in the room watched as Griggs retrieved his scalpel and bleeding bowl from the bag he carried. Ruth knew that although the practice of bleeding patients was becoming out of fashion, Doctor Griggs was an old man and his education had been learned in London. Ruth had heard her parents say that some people in the Village considered Doctor Griggs to be too outdated to be effective, but he was the only doctor the Village had.

Tituba suddenly spoke, and every face in the room turned to look at her.

"Betty be needing herbs," Tituba said, "and I have herbs. I gather healing herbs from the woods. I have medicine to make the child sleep. Sleep will give her body a chance to mend. No bleeding."

The room was deathly quiet for a moment, but then the stillness was broken by Abigail's shouts. "Tituba's a witch!" she exclaimed. "She uses herbs to make witchcraft spells! I know what Tituba does, because I've seen her!"

The room was deathly quiet once again, this time because everyone seemed too shocked to react. Finally Reverend Parris asked, "Abigail, do you know what you're saying?"

Tituba ran from her place against the wall into the center of the room. Her hands were flung up to her face, and she was bent over forward as though suffering from some sort of internal pain. "I be no witch!" she cried passionately. "I learn healing medicines from Barbados. I be a healer, not a witch!"

Doctor Griggs sat up straight on Betty's bed. "Maybe a person can cure an illness because they know what the illness is, since they inflicted it in the first place."

Tituba still stood in the center of the room, towering over those who sat on Betty's bed. She looked at Doctor Griggs and said, "You cure illness, does that mean you inflict illness?"

"Slave, know your place!" bellowed Reverend Parris.

"I be asking Doctor Griggs, you cure illness, do you inflict illness?" Tituba persisted.

"I use scientific methods that are approved by the church and therefore approved by God," Griggs finally answered. "I use time-proven cures that are an accepted part of society. But you, well now, where did you get your herb ideas? To think that plants could cure disease is utter nonsense, unless the plants are used in magical potions, and then that would be Satan's work. And if that's the case here, then I have to ask you some more questions. Did you give Betty anything to make her act this way?"

"I gave Betty nothing," Tituba said. "I learned how to make medicine from my mama, back on the Island. In Barbados, people live off the land. The land is generous, gives the people good things."

"The land is just dirt," Reverend Parris interrupted. "It is God who gives people things. God is the giver, not the earth. You speak heathen thoughts, and I won't allow that sort of thing in my house. This is a God-fearing household. I am always on the lookout for Satan's evil influence, and I'm hearing it from you. Has Satan influenced you?"

Tituba backed up a step, and straightened her posture in surprise.

"I'm talking to you!" Parris suddenly bellowed. "Have you been listening to Satan?"

At that moment, Abigail went into a frenzy, shaking her body and rolling her eyes. "Yes!" Abigail cried, "Tituba listens to Satan! She's a witch! She put a spell on Betty, and now she's putting her evil eye on me too! Oh, she's pinching me from across the room! I can feel her hurting me! Stop her! Stop Tituba!"

Abigail's eyes rolled back into their sockets and she collapsed down upon her bed in a dead faint.

Chapter Five

Ruth was ordered to go back to her room.

She lay in her bed, seeing nothing in the darkness, but thinking a great deal. She was trying to mentally sort through all the events of the evening so she could understand not only what she had witnessed, but also what it all meant.

She decided to put different parts of the evening's extraordinary events into separate mental compartments so that she could analyze each portion individually.

She began with Betty's illness.

Ruth considered the symptoms and was sure she had never seen anything like it. She also remembered that Doctor Griggs had said he had never experienced such a dramatic display of symptoms in all his years of medical practice, either. She ran what she had witnessed over and over again in her mind, and became convinced that there was no play-acting on Betty's part. The illness was genuine. But what was it? What was wrong with Betty?

Then there was Abigail.

Abigail had displayed symptoms belatedly. Could she have watched long enough to ascertain Betty's behavior, and then tried to imitate it?

Was Abigail faking?

If so, why?

The answers were easy. If Abigail was faking her symptoms, it was because she wanted to seek revenge upon Tituba.

Ruth remembered that when she had first entered Betty's bedroom that evening, Abigail had said to the servantmaid, "You should have been a lot nicer to me." By accusing Tituba of witchcraft, Abigail had created a dire, even dangerous, situation for the servantmaid.

And—pretending an illness, especially such a dramatic illness, would be an ideal way for a disturbed child to receive attention.

Could in her own deranged way, Abigail be jealous of the attention that Betty had received as the result of the younger child's illness? Could Abigail have felt that Betty had one-upped her, so she thought she needed to pull the attention back to herself?

Then there was Tituba to consider. Was the servantmaid really a witch, or was it simply that she behaved differently because she originated from a far-away, exotic Island?

Still, when thinking about Tituba, Ruth's mind kept going back to the fact that she had heard John call his wife a sinner. That was powerful evidence against Tituba, indeed.

But Tituba had denied she was a witch, instead insisting that she was a healer, using herbs to do so. Ruth knew that some plants did cure illness. An example was peppermint, which Ruth's own mother had given her during times of a stomach upset. Doctor Griggs certainly must have known about the plant peppermint. Then why was he so adamant about saying that plants cannot cure illnesses?

Sighing, Ruth turned over in her bed, pulling the quilts up to her chin. She tried to listen to any sounds coming from the bedroom next to her own, but all was quiet.

She was just drifting off to sleep, when a loud pounding came upon her door and John Indian announced from the other side, "It be time to get up."

Ruth opened her eyes, thinking that she had gotten no sleep at all. It would be a long day ahead. She realized it was Sunday, and wondered if Reverend Parris would still preach or if the situation with his only child merited a change from the normal attendance at the church.

But she knew with all her being that Reverend Parris would never deviate from his agenda. He was a man of fierce commitment to his schedules. So Ruth resigned herself that she would be caring for the Village children, and therefore she had better get out of bed and get ready to do so.

She rose and quickly put on her day clothes. She was anxious to find out any news about Betty's condition. Ruth went out her bedroom into the landing, but the door to the children's' bedroom was closed and no one emerged. So she continued down to the dining room where Reverend Parris was already waiting at the table, Bible in hand.

"How is Betty?" Ruth asked as she sat at her place.

"She has a fever," Parris responded, "but Doctor Griggs has bled her. He left early this morning. Abigail is resting as well."

Ruth looked around, but only John was seated at the table, awaiting the morning Bible study. "Where's Tituba?" she asked.

"You shouldn't ask questions," Parris said curtly, "because children should be seen and not heard. You have no manners. But I'll tell you anyway: Tituba is confined to her room."

"Why?" Ruth persisted.

"You are insolent," Parris said, wiping his eyes, which were bleary from lack of sleep. "You should only speak when spoken to."

Parris opened the Bible and began to read from it: "But He shall say, I tell you, I know you not whence ye are; depart from me, all ye workers of iniquity."

He stopped reading and looked at Ruth and John. "There is iniquity even inside the house of a man of God; there is an abomination among us. But it shall be found and eliminated. God has given me the task to stop Satan's evil."

Reverend Parris began to read again. Eventually he closed the Bible.

"Now we'll go to the church," Parris informed Ruth, "and although no one is allowed to work on the Sabbath, God's work is the only exception. God's work is always needed. In Luke it is asked: 'Is it lawful to heal on the Sabbath Day? And they held their peace. And He took him, and healed him, and let it go.' So we will go to church today as we do all Sundays. We need God's protection against Satan's evil, because now Satan has come to Salem Village."

Ruth rose and went upstairs to collect her things. When she was ready, she came back downstairs, but the dining room was empty. Spying a loaf of rye bread still sitting on the kitchen table, she mused that since Tituba was not allowed out of her room, no one would put away that bread. So Ruth picked it up herself.

She hesitated for just a moment, but then entered the kitchen. She was relieved to discover that no one was in the room. But then she felt a prickling sensation like she was being watched, so she looked around.

There, standing in the servants' stairwell, holding the door open, was John Indian. His dark skin was so clean that it shone, and his eyes were like soft velvet. His hair was cropped close to his skull, and he stood tall and ramrod straight, his muscled body taking up the entire space in the stairwell entrance.

"Hello, John," Ruth greeted him. She decided to ask him some things. "Why is Tituba confined to her room?"

"Tituba be a sinner," John said, and stepped into the kitchen.

"Why would you say that?" Ruth asked.

"Because she sinned."

Well, Ruth thought, *this sure isn't getting me anywhere.*

John went to the kitchen sink and began putting away the breakfast utensils.

"Are you saying you believe that your wife is a witch?" Ruth got to the point.

John stopped his duties, seeming surprised. He looked at her for a moment as though appraising her. Then he looked away and continued sorting the utensils. "No," he said, "no witch. Tituba be a healer."

"Why then would you say that Tituba sinned?"

"Because she did."

Exasperated, Ruth tried again. "How did Tituba sin?"

"They are sins of the father," John said.

"What do you mean by that?" Ruth asked.

But before John could answer, the kitchen door burst open

and Reverend Parris walked in the room. "Get your outerwear on and let's go to the church," he barked his command at Ruth. "You've been wasting time."

"No, I haven't wasted time," Ruth protested, "because I've been putting the bread away."

"If I say you've wasted time, then you have wasted time!" shouted Parris.

Ruth fled for the front door, where she grabbed her coat and put it on. Reluctantly she faced the Reverend. When they left the Parris house, they walked in silence. They reached the entranceway of the church and once again Ruth removed and hung up her outerwear.

"Children should be seen and not heard," Reverend Parris repeated what he had told Ruth at the breakfast table. "That not only goes for you, but also for the Village children for whom you will be caring. Don't let me hear a sound when the children arrive. Now go and wait in the back room. The congregation will be here shortly."

Always glad to be rid of Parris, Ruth fled into the back room. She shut the door, which divided the children's room from the church. She felt relieved to be able to have some peace and quiet, even if only for a while. She sat on a stool and tried to relax.

Alone in the back room, she felt very serene for the first time in days. She was grateful for the brief respite from all of the bizarre happenings of the Parris household. She sat on a wooden stool in the empty children's room and drank in the stillness.

She contemplated her situation. In the Parris household, Ruth lived among people who were suspicious and sometimes even cruel, and she vowed to herself that none of these things would rub off on her by association. She realized there were times when she felt as though her heart would break, and that this situation was too much to bear on her shoulders, all by herself.

Ruth found herself wishing she had a friend. Even one single friend.

She sighed, and continued to sit quietly on a stool in the back room of the church. She wished the children would never show up, and that she would never have to go back to the Parris household when church services were over. So many things to wish for.

Suddenly the silence was broken by a tapping sound. Jumping up, Ruth looked wildly around the room. Calming her rapidly beating heart, she decided that someone must be tapping on the door that divided the back room from the church.

She walked to the door and slowly opened it. Sticking her head out, she realized that no one was on the other side. She glanced rapidly around the inside of the church and saw that Reverend Parris was standing at the pulpit, reading his prepared text, and was oblivious to her.

No one had been knocking on the door. So she shut it and stepped back inside the empty children's room.

Suddenly she heard the tapping sound again. Looking around, Ruth finally determined that the sound was coming from the only window in the room.

She was a little apprehensive, but curiosity overcame her hesitation and she walked to the window. She peered through the frosty panes of glass and then in surprise, she cried an unbidden, "Oh!"

There was William Porter, standing in the snow outside the window, grinning mischievously. He motioned to her that she should open the window.

Ruth couldn't resist, even knowing that if Reverend Parris should chose that moment to come into the back room, she would surely be whipped. But she was so happy to see William, and was heartened to see someone who was glad to see her in return. Maybe, just maybe, Ruth thought, at last she had found a friend.

She tugged on the window sash, as it was stuck in place. Finally, with much effort, the window came up and she could speak to William.

"Hello!" she said, "I'm glad to see you."

"You are?" William smiled even wider. "Even though by now you know who I am?"

"You can't help where you were born any more than I can,"

Ruth told him, still leaning on the window sill, oblivious to the cold. "Besides, you're the first friendly face I've seen in what seems like a long time."

"Well, I can imagine that's the truth!" he laughed and Ruth's heart soared. "The Parris's really *are* a bunch of sourpusses, aren't they?"

"Shhh!" Ruth scolded. "Someone could hear you."

"You're right; some people really don't like hearing the truth, do they?"

"What are you doing here?" Ruth changed the subject, knowing she didn't have much time.

"Talking to you," William answered.

"No," she said, "I mean, why are you here?"

"Because I wanted to talk to you," William said, and Ruth thought, *This is almost as round-about as that conversation I had with John Indian.*

"How did you know I'd be here?" Ruth asked.

"Everybody knows everybody's business in Salem Village," he said.

"I can imagine that's true," she said, then added, "listen, we can't be seen talking here. As a matter of fact, considering our last names, we can't be seen talking together anywhere."

"Can I meet you later this afternoon?" William asked.

"Where?"

"Doesn't Parris have a barn in back?" he asked. When she nodded, he said, "Meet me there today at three o'clock. I'll be waiting inside. I just want to talk to you, that's all. I'm perfectly harmless."

"I can't meet you in a barn!" Ruth exclaimed. "It wouldn't be proper!"

"Well, I'll be there at three," he turned and started to walk away, speaking over his shoulder, "and I hope you'll be there too. See you then!"

Ruth quickly shut the window, trying to be quiet so it wouldn't slam down upon the sill. Then she stood gazing out the window, watching William Porter walk away.

Chapter Six

Ruth felt elated to have talked to William.

At the same time, she was anxious because she had such mixed emotions about him. On one hand, she was aware that she was attracted to him and he moved her in such a way that she had never before experienced. And William must like her, or else why would he have sought her out?

But on the other hand, she knew that if she did decide to see him, it would be putting herself in a situation wrought with potential danger. She was aware that Puritan traditions required that young men and women were to be formally introduced by respected elders of the community. All courtships were to be supervised. To take it upon herself to meet William in a barn, of all places, was too immoral to even consider.

But Ruth was lonely. She wanted to do it.

Could she do it? Could she find the courage to do something as daring and as dangerous as to meet a young man secretly, in an unsupervised place?

And that was not even bringing into consideration that she was a Putnam and William was a Porter. What would her father say if he knew that she was considering meeting William Porter in a barn?

Oh! It was too scandalous to even consider.

But she wanted to do it.

Ruth heard sounds coming from inside the church, and she realized that the congregation was arriving. She moved quickly away from the window so that no one could have an inkling that anything out of the ordinary had just happened. She sat on a stool, and tried to act perfectly bland.

The door burst open and a woman wearing layers of black clothing entered, carrying an infant and being trailed by other youngsters. Soon she was joined by other women, all dressed from chin to toe in dark, somber clothing. The only bright spots on their dresses were the starched white cowls and the starched white sleeves of their formal church attire. Ruth understood that vanity was a sin, and therefore the women of Salem Village took great care to direct attention away from their appearance.

Before long, she was surrounded by small children, who all seemed to be either crying or crawling. She realized that to care for these children was a big job, and by the time the church services were started, she was already exhausted.

As always, the service lasted hours. Finally, after what seemed to be an eternity, the somberly dressed women came back into the room to collect their children once again. When all had left, Ruth collapsed on the stool where she normally sat. Her hair had tumbled out of her severe bun to hang in strands around her face, and her dress was rumpled and soiled.

The door opened, and Reverend Parris gestured to Ruth that she should come out. "You'll clean this room tomorrow," he told her, "but today you need to get back home to see how Betty and Abby are faring."

As Ruth trudged behind Parris through the snow, she couldn't help but glare at him out of the corner of her eye. She blamed him for her unhappy fate.

Once home, she was eager for news of Betty and Abigail, and she knocked on the closed door leading to the children's room. Summoned inside, Ruth entered. She saw immediately that Betty was still a very sick child. Pale and sweating, Betty's hair fell in wet rivulets down her face. She appeared to be sleeping, but Ruth wasn't sure if that was the situation or if the child was unconscious.

In contrast, Abigail sat straight up in her bed, still wearing her woolen nightdress.

Reverend Parris was standing at the foot of Betty's bed, his arms crossed and his face concerned.

"How are you, Abigail?" Ruth asked, and sat on Abigail's bed.

"Terrible, just terrible," Abigail cried. "I am being bewitched! Tituba is a witch! She pinches me! She sends evil spirits to punish me because I won't write my name in Satan's book!"

"Tell me more about Satan's book," Reverend Parris encouraged his niece.

Ruth turned to face him. "How can you listen to this? How can you believe her?"

"Know thy place!" Parris bellowed, and Ruth cringed back upon the bed. Then he turned back to Abigail and gently prompted, "Go on, child; you're with me, and I am a man of God. You need not be afraid to tell the truth."

Ruth saw that all of the Reverend's attention was focused upon Abigail. *She's getting what she wants,* Ruth thought to herself; *Abigail is finally getting the attention she craves from her Uncle.*

But she felt helpless to intervene.

"It's so awful," Abigail told her uncle. "In the middle of the night, Tituba sent a yellow bird to peck at me and to torment me. Then when you were in church, Tituba sent her own spirit into my bedroom. She was still in her own room, yet she sent in a ghost of herself. And that ghost was holding a book full of signatures. Uncle Parris, Tituba wanted me to sign my soul to Satan! She told me that Betty had refused to sign in the same book, and look what happened to *her*! So I'm afraid for myself. Oh, please don't let Tituba hurt me like she's doing Betty! You must protect me."

"I *will* protect you," Reverend Parris soothed his niece. He sat on her bed next to Ruth, and Abigail leaned towards him. Abigail took his hand in hers.

Ruth rose and moved to sit on Betty's bed. She glanced briefly at the stricken young girl, and saw that Betty still remained pale and motionless, appearing like a tiny bundle underneath the blankets. Betty seemed to be very sick, indeed.

"Uncle Parris," Abigail continued, "you should know that it's not just Tituba who is doing the devil's work. There are others."

Appearing shocked, the Reverend sat up ram-rod straight. "Do you know who they are?"

"I got up in the middle of the night. I looked out the window. I saw Goody Good dancing in our yard at midnight."

"The beggarwoman?" Reverend gasped.

"Yes, the beggarwoman," Abigail confirmed. "Dancing is the devil's doing. It is a sin to dance."

Reverend Parris squeezed Abigail's hand, and Ruth noticed the hungry look on Abigail's face. "I'll get the Village Magistrate," he said, "and we'll get to the bottom of this. I think it's becoming a legal matter. We need to interrogate these followers of Satan and stop them from hurting any more children. Betty is not suffering from an illness; instead, she is suffering from a witchcraft hex. This is assault and attempted murder by witches. If Tituba and Goody Good are guilty, then they can hang for these charges."

Suddenly he let go of Abigail's hand and rose to stand. "We must put an end to the spread of Satan's evil influences!" he bellowed. "We must hold those evildoers responsible and make them confess their sins!"

"Wait!" Ruth cried. "Think about what you're doing! Abigail just wants attention!"

"Then how do you explain what happened to Betty?" Abigail sat up in bed and spat out her question to Ruth. "You can't explain it, but I can! I am the only one who knows the truth, because I've seen Tituba and Sarah Good do Satan's work! They are witches!"

Then Abigail's arm rose from beneath her blankets, and she pointed her index finger at Ruth. "Why would you deny the truth?" she accused Ruth. "Are you denying the truth because you have something to hide?"

Horrified and afraid, Ruth's first instinct was to deny the charges and therefore protect herself from the madness that surrounded her in this room. "No!" she cried. "I am a good, God-fearing person!"

Seemingly satisfied with Ruth's obvious fear, Abigail turned again to face her uncle. "But Tituba is from a heathen land," she reminded him, "and Goody Good hasn't been to church services for two weeks."

"That's true," Reverend Parris mused, "so that makes me wonder how long Satan has been in Salem Village. Satan wouldn't dare enter the house of God, so it had to have been two weeks then, because he's associated with Goody Good. So that beggarwoman has been doing Satan's work for two weeks. How could I have missed Satan's entry into Salem? I will take care of it now, though, and put a stop to Satan's evil."

With that, the Reverend turned on his heels. "Stay and watch the girls," he instructed to Ruth as he walked out of the bedroom.

Still sitting on Betty's bed, Ruth looked at Abigail. "Do you realize what you're doing?"

"Well, it *could* be Satan," Abigail smirked.

"I want to know," Ruth spoke quietly, "if Tituba is a witch or not."

"Maybe she is, and maybe she isn't. Maybe I'm lying, and maybe I'm not."

"This is no game," Ruth said. "The people you're accusing could be hanged if the Village magistrate believes your stories."

"And so what if they are?" Abigail was still sitting upright in her bed. "Tituba is a Negress. Who cares about her? She should have been nice to me. She was always nice to Betty! Why couldn't she have been nice to me, too? And Sarah Good, well, she's just a beggerwoman so that's another one nobody cares about. And besides, Goody Good wasn't nice to me either, so she deserves whatever she gets, too."

"I believe you're doing this so that your uncle will pay attention to you," Ruth quietly accused. "But no amount of attention is worth innocent people's lives. Please, please think about what you're doing."

"I've thought about it," Abigail said, and her voice was brittle. "No one loves me. My father died and my mother abandoned me. But my uncle wants me enough to have me in his household. Uncle Parris is the only one that wants me at all. I love him."

"Abigail," Ruth tried to remain calm, "again, please reconsider. It's not healthy to be thinking these types of thoughts."

"Uncle Parris is the only one in the world who likes me," Abigail continued adamantly. "Everyone else hates me. I think that if I helped him to get rid of Satan's influences out of Salem Village, my uncle will be very happy with me."

"Abigail—" Ruth began.

Abigail interrupted. "Not only would I be earning my uncle's love, but I'd be getting rid of my enemies, too."

"Even if your enemies are innocent?"

"Who cares?" Abigail shrugged her shoulders. "Tituba and Goody Good should have thought about that when they were mean to me. And you," Abigail pointed at Ruth, "you'd better take my side in all of this. Because if you don't, I'll tell my uncle that you're a witch, too!"

Ruth felt a chill of fear. "You wouldn't!"

"Don't ever think I wouldn't," Abigail narrowed her small, dark eyes.

"Why would Reverend Parris believe you?" Ruth asked.

"For a couple of reasons," Abigail said. "First of all, I'm family. Why wouldn't anyone believe his or her own family? Secondly, Uncle Parris is always at risk for losing his job, because a lot of people here don't like him. Of course, he thinks that Satan is influencing the Villagers against him. What I'm telling him about witches is only helping him believe that Satan is out to get him. But I'm really doing this because the Villagers are mean to my uncle. Just like the Villagers are mean to me. You see, I know how it feels not to be liked. So by helping Uncle Parris, I am going to get revenge against *everybody*."

"And as for you," Abigail glared at Ruth, "well, you'd better decide which side you'll be on, because I'm still deciding what to do with you. If you want to be my friend, well, I'd like to have a friend. But you'd better stay away from my uncle."

Ruth understood the enormity of the situation. She felt fear into the very marrow of her bones. She knew she had to be very, very careful around Abigail. "If I became your friend," Ruth chose her words carefully, "what would it mean?"

"You'd have to talk to me," Abigail said, "and you couldn't make fun of me. You'd have to keep my secrets. But most of all, you could never be mean to me."

"What kind of secrets do you have?"

Abigail reached under her blanket. "Here's one," she said, and pulled out a cloth doll. The doll was unevenly stitched, and appeared lopsided as a result. The doll wore a colorful piece of cloth as a shift-dress. The shift-dress was sewn directly onto the body so that it couldn't be removed unless the stitches were cut.

"What's so secret about a doll?" Ruth asked.

"It's a secret," was all Abigail would say.

More than a little worried, Ruth was silent. She glanced around the room, then looked out the window. Suddenly she realized how late in the afternoon it had gotten to be.

William would be waiting out in the barn for her.

She wondered how she could find a way to go outside without anyone seeing her.

She began forming a plan, because Ruth had decided that she did want to meet William Porter in the barn after all.

Chapter Seven

"I have to attend to the baking in the kitchen," Ruth suddenly blurted.

"You're supposed to watch me and Betty," Abigail pouted, as she once again tucked the cloth doll underneath the covers of the bed where she sat.

"I'll come back in about an hour," Ruth promised, "and then I'll stay with you all night. In fact, I'll bring up your supper so you can eat in your room."

"Well," Abigail said dubiously, "I suppose."

Relieved that it had been so easy, she jumped up from Betty's bed. With a backward glance at the small child who was so desperately ill, Ruth's heart moved in sympathy. Was Betty going to die?

Well, Ruth thought to herself, *I'll be back in an hour to take care of her.*

She entered the hallway. Hesitating, Ruth impulsively decided to take the servant's stairwell instead of the main one. The servant's stairs went directly to the kitchen and exited very close to the back door. It was true what Abigail had once said; the servant's stairwell was for secret things, and if anything were ever a secret thing, it would be this.

Ruth's heart pounded in her chest and she could hear its beating in her ears. She carefully opened the second-story door to the stairwell, hoping it wouldn't creak. The darkness of the interior was intimidating, but she was determined to continue. Shaking slightly, Ruth stepped into the narrow entranceway.

The stairs were not very visible in the gloom, so she kept her hands on both walls for support and for balance. Remembering how steep the stairs were, she had to move slowly, even though her mind silently screamed for her to hurry, hurry, or she could get caught.

She concentrated on putting one foot carefully in front of the other, and suddenly she realized she was holding her breath. She let her breath out slowly, not wanting to make even the slightest sound. Her heart skipped a beat when her winter cloak rustled with her movements, and she stopped for a moment, hesitating in apprehension.

Ruth removed her hands from the walls and, because she was shaking with nerves, she teetered on the edge of a steep step. Then she collected her balance and used her hands to pull her cloak tighter around her shoulders to silence the noise. She froze in dismay when a button popped from the outerwear and clattered down the steep steps.

Frightened, Ruth knew that losing the button was unavoidable at this point. And there would be no searching for it at the bottom of the dark stairwell. The button would have to remain wherever it fell.

Trying to breathe normally, Ruth once again began her descent down the steep stairs. Her eyes were adjusting to the gloom and she felt more confident. She arrived at the bottom and reached for the knob of the door that would open into the kitchen.

Again Ruth hesitated as the adrenaline coursed through her veins. What if someone was in the kitchen? How would she know unless she opened the door to look? But once she opened the door, it would be too late. If someone were in the kitchen, she would be caught.

Her mind searched for answers. But then she made a decision. She would open the door and go into the kitchen. If the kitchen were occupied, then she would say she was looking for food to bring to Abigail.

Her mind whispered: *Isn't lying a sin?*

Her staunch Puritan upbringing haunted Ruth, but she felt driven to see William. It was almost a compulsion. She wanted to talk to somebody who was nice, and whom she liked. Ruth realized that she was desperately unhappy because she had been so incredibly lonely in the strange Parris household.

To find a friend would be worth any price.

Ruth turned the doorknob, and the door from the servants' stairwell creaked open. Timidly Ruth put her head through so she could see into the kitchen. The brightness of the room in contrast to the gloomy stairwell almost hurt her eyes. But then she looked, and sighed in relief, because the kitchen was empty of any people.

She entered the kitchen, then carefully closed the stairwell door behind her. Scampering lightly, she reached the back door leading to the yard. Ruth took a deep breath, then tugged the door open, feeling the bite of cold air on her face. Quickly she exited the kitchen, shutting the door and turning to race across the back yard.

Would anyone be looking out a window right at that moment?

Ruth's heart pounded and she could barely catch her breath. She couldn't ever remember feeling so afraid. She ran as fast as she could towards the barn. The length of the yard seemed so much longer than it really was. The time it took to reach the barn seemed endless.

But at last she reached it.

Breathing hard, Ruth entered the barn. The smell of manure assaulted her nostrils, and she had trouble seeing in the dim light. She could hear a horse moving in its stall. Was William here? What if he didn't show up? What if he never intended to meet her at all? Was she taking this incredible risk for nothing?

But then a shape stepped out of a dim corner, and Ruth's apprehension changed to a nervousness of a different sort. What would she say to him? What would he think of a young woman who so risqué that she would meet a man in an unsupervised environment? Would he think her too bold, and too brazen to be respected?

Ruth was anxiously trying to think of something to say, but William spoke first.

"I knew you'd come," he said, stepping nearer to her, "and

I'm so glad you did."

Startled, Ruth asked, "You are? Glad I'm here, I mean?"

She could see him now that her eyes adjusted to the gloomy interior of the Parris barn. He stood in front of her, and Ruth could see how handsome he was. He had a strong chin and a straight nose. But it was his eyes that attracted her the most; they were large, brown and deep, and framed with dark lashes.

"Yes, I'm very glad to be with you," he grinned.

He reached for her hand, and she felt short of breath at his touch. Her thoughts became jumbled and she couldn't sort through anything in her mind. Part of her still called to her that this was wrong, so very wrong; but then any ability to reason fled from her so she dismissed every message her brain attempted so send. She became numb, subject only to feelings, not thoughts.

This was the forbidden fruit, and she wanted so desperately to taste it.

Suddenly she wanted to rebel against Reverend Parris, against her father, and against all of her Puritan upbringing. She found herself squeezing William's hand as a gesture to show that she was a willing participant. She silently sent a message that she wouldn't pull away.

He pulled her hand with his own, and led her to a tightly bound bale of fragrant, fresh hay. He sat down upon it and, still pulling her hand, gently tugging at her until Ruth had to decide to either sit beside him or let go of his hand.

She chose to sit.

William released her hand, but moved closer to her until he was touching her knee with his own. Fear of sin and feelings of guilt nagged at Ruth, but again she was able to suppress her misgivings.

What was happening right then in the Parris barn was the most exciting thing she had ever experienced in her entire life, and she was enraptured. The whole idea titillated her and she found herself unable to stop her longings to be with this man.

"I'm worried about you," William told her.

She felt a thrill that finally, someone cared about her. Still, it was hardly the sort of thing she expected him to say.

"Why are you worried?" she asked, very conscious of his knee still touching hers as they sat together on the hay.

"I think you ought to leave the Parris household," William said.

She turned to look at him. "I've nowhere else to go."

"Parris is a fanatic," William told her. "His mind is not right. He sees Satan lurking in every dark corner. I think he only sees a reflection of himself."

Ruth gasped. "You can't say that about a man of God!" she exclaimed.

He turned to her. "Remember, only recently has Parris become a man of God. Not very long ago, he was simply a failed businessman. I question his commitment to our Lord. Frankly, I'm wondering if Parris might even prove to be a fraud."

Ruth studied the walls of the barn, noticing how the weak winter sun streamed through the cracks in the boards, creating a striped effect. "Well, he does seem a bit extreme."

"I'm afraid you might not be safe in the Parris household," William said.

"Why wouldn't I be safe?"

"Rumors are flying that there is going to be a big political change here in Salem Village, and that Parris is getting desperate," William said. "There is another man who should be appointed minister of Salem Village. A *real* man of God, not an impostor like Parris."

"Politics have nothing to do with me," Ruth was genuinely puzzled. "And who is this other man?"

"Ruth," William continued, ignoring her question, "you could get caught up in what's going to happen by association. You might wind up in the middle just because of where you are living. Parris has been acting very strangely lately and some Villagers have been saying that he's gone over the edge. I think there's going to be a power struggle in the near future. I don't want you involved."

"These things are between the Reverend and the Village

Council," Ruth said, "so even if what you are saying did happen, it couldn't affect me."

"You have no idea of what is going to happen. Tell your father you want to go back home."

"I can't," Ruth said softly, and her voice trembled, "because it was my father's wish that I be here. I can't disobey my father."

"Your father feels he owes Parris a debt," William said, "but that debt should not be paid through you."

She turned to look at him once again. "What? What debt?"

"Never mind," William said. Then, suddenly he said, "Ruth, I like you very much."

But before she could react to his words, William put his arm around her shoulder. She looked up in amazement, and he used that as an opportunity to kiss her lips while her face was turned towards him.

Startled, Ruth jerked in a surprised spasm, and her lips were momentarily bruised against his teeth. She gasped and jumped up off of the bale of hay.

He had kissed her!

All of the constraints of her Puritan upbringing came back to her in a rush. She couldn't believe that, outside of wedlock, a man had actually kissed her.

She stood there for a moment, looking down at William who remained sitting. Too stunned to speak, Ruth suddenly whirled around and fled towards the door of the barn.

"I'll see you again soon!" William called after her. "I'll find you!"

But Ruth continued to run, making a mad dash back to the Parris household. She reached the heavy wooden door of the back of the house, and found herself trembling so violently that she almost couldn't turn the doorknob. But finally it twisted in her hand and Ruth entered the kitchen.

And there she found herself face-to-face with Abigail Williams.

Abigail was still wearing her woolen nightdress. She gazed at Ruth with her small, dark eyes, unblinking. Her arm was outstretched. Gradually Abigail unfolded her fingers to reveal something in her hand.

It was Ruth's button, retrieved from the servants' stairwell.

"Abigail," Ruth was white with fear, "I can explain."

"Maybe I'd believe whatever you'd tell me, or maybe I wouldn't," Abigail said slowly. "Maybe I'll keep this a secret, or maybe I won't. You're not sure what I'll do, are you?"

"Abigail…" Ruth trailed off.

"Get me something to eat," Abigail suddenly commanded. "Bring it upstairs. And you can bring something for Betty to eat, too. Because Betty woke up."

Chapter Eight

"All rise."

Ruth rose to her feet, listening to the shuffling sounds as people in the packed courtroom got off the wooden benches that served as spectator seats. Others were standing in the back; an overflow of people, as the room's seating capacity had been more than maximized.

The idea of a witch trial was exciting to the Villagers; tantalizing the inhabitants, so almost everyone from the Village was in attendance, all craning their necks for a better view.

The court's magistrate entered the room, and everyone strained to see him.

Sounds permeated. Ruth could hear sniffing and coughing because the season of respiratory illnesses was upon them. She heard a baby fussing, and she heard the mother attempting to pacify the child. Somebody in the courtroom was sobbing softly, so softly that Ruth almost missed it. But yes, someone was crying, and it didn't sound like a child.

She looked at her surroundings. The Village hall was small, and with so many people in attendance, the room was warmed by body heat, even though it was the first day of March. The unyielding wooden pews were jammed with spectators, and in front of the seating area was a dark wooden railing, almost as though to hold people back.

There was no jury. There was a wooden platform in front, and upon it was the box for the magistrate to sit and reign over the courtroom. Directly alongside the magistrate's chair was the witness chair, upon which Tituba Indian now sat.

The magistrate seated himself and the spectators followed suit and also sat, creating more shuffling and rustling sounds as they settled back upon the wooden benches. The magistrate wore a long black robe and upon his head was a large, powdered-white wig. The wig was worn like a hat, for it did not cover his entire head. He was an old man, and a prominent nose jutted out from his face, which otherwise appeared drawn and wrinkled, almost sunk in upon itself.

"Hear ye," the magistrate spoke, and everyone became instantly silent. No one wanted to miss a minute of this exciting event. "You all know me. I am John Hathorne. This court is composed of freemen from Salem Village. This is a trial where the accusers shall give witness. The accusers are Abigail Williams and Mary Walcott."

Ruth wondered why Mary Walcott was suddenly considered an accuser, but remained silent. Mary was a neighbor of the Parris', seventeen years old, and she was seated further down in the front row. Mary was a plain child that usually went unnoticed by others, but she was certainly in the limelight now.

Hathorne continued, "Three persons are hereby accused of witchcraft. The three persons are Tituba Indian, Sarah Good, and Sarah Osborne. These three accused will have to prove their innocence or else they will be judged as guilty. Conviction means death by hanging."

Ruth gasped. Death by hanging.

And when had Goody Osborne been accused? Ruth tried to recall who Sarah Osborne was. Then she remembered that Goody Osborne was a widow who had remarried. Except that the second man Osborne had married was the hired hand from her farm.

She knew that Goody Osborne's choice of a field hand for a husband had placed the woman in a position to be scorned by the other inhabitants of Salem Village. Ruth thought about this, and realized that Sarah Osborne was another woman who was considered in low regard by the rest of the community, just like Tituba and Goody Sarah Good. It seemed that a pattern was forming as to the type of citizen that was chosen to be accused of witchcraft.

Hathorne spoke to the courtroom with flair, his booming voice easily projecting throughout the room. "What is happening in Salem Village right now is not the first incidence of a witch attempting to corrupt a fine upstanding community. We have documentation of this type of extraordinary event, as chronicled in a book that was published three years ago about a witch in Boston."

The crowd murmured at this news.

Hathorne continued, "The community where that evil woman lived was only cleansed from Satan's influences through her death. The book to which I am referring is titled *Memorable Providences Relating to Witches and Possessions*. This important book was written by the renowned Reverend Cotton Mather, who, as you all know, is the revered clergyman of the South Church of Boston. This book can instruct the court about how to proceed to cleanse this village from Satan's influences. The court will follow the guidance of this book and will refer to it as needed."

Hathorne cleared his throat, then said, "We will begin by interrogating Tituba Indian, as she was the first to be accused." He turned to face the black servantmaid who sat and trembled alongside his bench. "Slave, what have you to say for yourself? Speak up!"

Ruth was shocked at Tituba's appearance. Gone was the stately, exotic elegance that Tituba had exuded the entire time that Ruth had known her. In its place, Tituba cowered in the witness chair, trembling and fearful. The colorful scarves she had always worn on her head were absent, and in contrast, her hair was bound in a plain cloth, once white but now dingy from use without washing. Tituba's face, once radiant, was now drawn and haggard, and for the first time, her age was obvious.

Ruth realized how awful it must have been for Tituba, confined to her bedroom to contemplate her fate all alone. A few days prior, Tituba's husband John had moved into an empty bedroom without his wife.

And Ruth could understand how it felt to be all alone.

But she knew that she could never comprehend how it must feel to be in fear for her very life. Ruth's heart went out to Tituba, for she could not find it within herself to believe that the servantmaid would ever have harmed Betty, who was only treated with kindness by the black woman who now sat, accused, on the witness chair.

"Slave, answer to these charges of witchcraft!" the magistrate commanded.

"I be no witch," Tituba whispered.

"Slave, speak up!" cried Hathorne. Then without waiting for her to do as he commanded, he turned to face the crowded courtroom, and said, "Reverend Parris, you may question the accused."

Ruth held her breath as beside her, Parris rose. He strolled, almost leisurely, to the front of the courtroom until he was standing directly in front of Tituba.

"Why do you hurt these poor children?" Parris suddenly blurted, his voice so loud that Tituba visibly jumped in her chair.

"I never hurt any children."

"You torment these children!" Parris bellowed. "See what you have done! You have caused great illness. Who commands you to hurt these children?"

"I never hurt any children," Tituba repeated, and Ruth thought she saw the servantmaid's eyes glisten.

"Do you admit to being a witch?"

"I know nothing of witches."

"If you know nothing of witches," Parris countered, "then how do you know if you are a witch or not? If you don't know about witches, how can you be sure *you* are not a witch?"

"I…" Tituba seemed confused at the question. "I don't understand. I don't know wot you want me to say."

"I want you to say who commands you to hurt these children!" Parris yelled. "You hurt them because they refuse to sign Satan's book!"

Suddenly, right beside Ruth, Abigail jumped off the wooden bench and stood up. "Tituba scratches me," she wailed. "Tituba sends ghosts to pinch me in the middle of the night. Sometimes the spirits bite me when I try to sleep. Tituba makes her witchcraft spells to hurt me. She has put a witchcraft spell on me right now. Stop her! Stop Tituba!"

As if on cue, Mary Walcott, seated further down in the front row, also rose to her feet.

"Witch! Witch! Witch!" Both girls began chanting in unison, gaining in pitch until it became a frenzied screeching. They shuddered and quaked elaborately, and waived their arms above their heads in circular motions. Their eyes rolled in their sockets and spittle formed at their mouths. The two girls created a tremendous spectacle for the Villagers in attendance, all of whom were morbidly fascinated with the demonstrations of apparent demonic possession.

Tituba rose to her feet. "I be no witch!"

"Slave!" the magistrate bellowed. "Sit back down."

Appearing dazed and bewildered, Tituba slowly backed down and sat down upon the witness chair. Tears coursed down her cheeks, but she cried silently, and did not bother to wipe away the tears. It was as though Tituba didn't even realize that she was crying.

For many more minutes, Abigail Williams and Mary Walcott continued their abhorrent displays of fiendish agitation. Not a person in the courtroom made any attempts to stop the frenzied demonstrations. The girls continued, unrestrained by any members of the court.

Ruth looked at Hathorne, and realized that the magistrate seemed to be just as fascinated with this performance as was everyone else in the room. Only Tituba appeared unmoved by the displays of the girls, and the servantmaid continued to cry silently.

Finally both girls seemed to tire, and slowly they decelerated their exhibitionist behavior. Gradually they grew less frantic and eventually they returned to their seats. Silence filled the small courtroom. Some spectators seemed to be in shock, while others appeared to be savoring the excitement of the day's events.

Then Parris once again turned to question Tituba. Surprisingly, this time his voice was soft.

"If you confess, it will be easier for you."

The servantmaid froze, then raised her eyes to meet those of the Reverend's.

"Wot?" she asked.

"I said," Parris still spoke softly, "if you tell the truth, then your sentence might be easier."

"But I told the truth," Tituba said. "I be no witch."

"You lie!" Parris suddenly bellowed at the top of his voice, and Tituba again jumped in her chair. So did most of the people in the courtroom, who had been leaning forward to hear Parris' words.

"I repeat," Parris continued, "if you confess, you might be judged with lenience, providing that you admit your sins and ask the Lord for His forgiveness. You must also confess who else in Salem Village is in league with the Devil. Because you have Satan's ear, that means you have privy to Satan's secrets."

Tituba blinked. "But how can I say I be a witch when I am no witch?"

"In Exodus, it says 'Thou shalt not suffer a witch to live.'" Parris took another step towards the witness chair, until he was merely a few feet in front of Tituba. "There is damning evidence against you."

"Wot evidence?"

"This!" Parris whipped something out of his pocket. He held it up, turning slowly around to face the courtroom so that all could see the object in his hand. It was a doll, a cloth doll. The entire crowd of spectators sighed collectively, and all strained to see this new and damning evidence.

"There is a pin in this doll!" Parris exclaimed, as he continued to hold the cloth doll up for the entire courtroom to see. Then he turned back to face Tituba. "I found this devil doll in your bedroom."

Ruth sat upright and gasped. She recognized it to be the same cloth doll that Abigail had showed her just the other night, the doll that Abigail had hidden underneath her bedsheets.

Without thinking, Ruth jumped up from her chair. "No!" she cried, and everyone looked at her in surprise. "No, that doll belongs to Abigail! It's not Tituba's!"

At that moment, Abigail also leaped from her seat, and began another fevered display of frenzied twitching and shaking. She began to sway, bumping into Ruth, and appeared as though she could topple over at any second.

Abigail shrieked nonsensical words and pointed at the ceiling. She then cried out, "I see a dark spirit on the rafters! It's a dark ghost of a man. He's sitting on the ceiling, on the rafters above Ruth. The ghost is pointing at Ruth. He wants Ruth to join the others and sign his evil book!"

Down the row, Mary Walcott jumped up from her seat and joined in, "I see him too! I see him too! He's pointing at Ruth!"

Abigail grabbed Ruth's arms, pinning them to her side. Ruth found that, for a twelve-year-old child, Abigail seemed exceedingly strong.

Ruth blanched and felt nausea threatening to overpower her, because she recognized that suddenly, the whole courtroom was looking at her and judging her. She was horrified at how quickly the course of events had suddenly twisted and were now aimed in her direction. She was deathly afraid, and realized that she very well should be afraid.

"Let me go," Ruth tried to break free of Abigail's grip.

"Resist the Devil!" Abigail cried, and Ruth instantly understood what was really at stake. Abigail was telling Ruth not to interfere.

Or else.

She felt adrenaline course through her veins, and thought, *What should I do? Should I take a risk and help Tituba?*

She turned her head to look at Tituba, who was sitting motionless and helpless on the stand. Tituba was gazing back, desperation and pleading apparent on her face. Part of Ruth wanted to help the servantmaid. But she felt an overwhelming fear, a fear so strong that she felt immobilized, and suddenly she discovered within herself an impassioned need for self-preservation.

She looked at Parris, who seemed to completely believe everything his niece said, no matter how outrageous the content. Ruth wondered, *If Abigail accused her along with the others, would Parris act upon his niece's accusations? Would he have her jailed, too, as a witch?*

Decide, decide!

"I was mistaken. That's not the same doll," Ruth called out, and she saw Tituba collapse into a heap, landing on the floor in a dead faint.

"Throw water on this slave," Hathorne instructed. The magistrate pointed his finger at the courtroom. "You, John Proctor, pick this slave off of the floor and throw water in her face. Revive the accused so that the trial may continue."

An elderly man rose from his seat in the second row and obeyed the orders of the magistrate. Parris stepped aside and let Proctor pass.

Ruth sat back down, dejected and ashamed. *How can I ever live with myself again?*

Abigail stopped shaking and said in a loud voice, "The dark spirit has vanished. Ruth is spared from Satan's influences."

Abigail remained standing for another minute or two while the courtroom came back to order. Everyone was excited but quickly became quiet once again when Tituba was revived and forced to sit back upon the witness chair. No one wanted to miss a moment of this extraordinary event.

What a show!

Ruth watched Parris. She thought that if he were a dog, he would be salivating. Parris addressed Abigail. "What did the ghost on the rafter look like?"

Abigail answered, "He's gone now."

"But what did he look like?" Parris persisted. "I want to be able to recognize Satan. Was it Satan himself sitting in this courtroom?"

"I don't know," Abigail said firmly. "He's gone now. I was

too afraid to look at him. I don't want to see Satan, I only want to see God."

With that, Abigail sat down, and the expression on the Reverend's face was one of extreme disappointment. Mary Walcott also sat, and temporarily, it seemed, order was restored in the courtroom.

"Slave," Parris turned to Tituba, and continued his interrogation, "what will you say about this doll?"

"I have not seen it before," Tituba whispered, looking weak from her faint.

"This evil doll was found in your bedroom."

"I don't know how it got there."

Parris tried another tactic. "You have put a spell on your own husband!"

Again the courtroom gasped in a collective reaction to this new evidence.

Parris whirled about and looked at his audience, who were the people of Salem Village. These people were actually listening to his words after so many Sundays of indifference. The Reverend appeared to be relishing the absolute attention he received from the people of this courtroom; the kind of attention that he had never received from his church congregation.

"My other slave, John Indian, is sick in bed," Parris informed the attentive crowd. "Yes, right now, he is sick. He has the same sickness that my Betty had. Thank God, Betty is getting better. But now John is sick. John Indian has been bewitched."

Pandemonium broke out in the courtroom at the receipt of this revelation. People gasped and exclaimed in surprise, and some made the sign of the cross over their breasts to protect themselves from evil.

Parris waited for the spectators to once again become calm. When the noise died down, he turned back to Tituba. "What do you say to the fact that your own husband now has the illness?"

"I cause no illness."

"What do you say to the fact that you have been seen gathering herbs in the forest?"

"I use herbs to heal. My mama in Barbados taught me to use herbs to heal."

"What do you say to the fact that Doctor Griggs can testify that it is impossible for plants to be used for any medicinal purposes?"

Parris glared at Tituba, who looked bewildered and didn't respond. Then he continued, "You say you're a healer. But don't you only cure those sicknesses that you cause? If you know what can cure those sicknesses, isn't it only because you caused the sicknesses in the first place? You don't heal, you just reverse the original spells you cast, don't you?"

Tituba cowered in her chair. "I cause no illness. I cause no sickness. I cast no spells."

Parris was silent for a moment, appearing to think. He turned to face the courtroom, then slowly walked towards the spectators until he was almost directly at the railing separating the Villagers from the courtroom proceedings.

Suddenly he whirled around to face Tituba once again, and bellowed, "Confess your sins! Slave, do you wish to hang?"

Tituba's tears freely flowed down her dark cheeks as she stared back at the minister, but she remained mute.

"Confess!" Parris strode back towards Tituba. "The evidence is overwhelmingly against you. If you confess your sins, perhaps the good Lord will take it upon Himself to forgive you. Perhaps you can find mercy. But you need to confess first. And—you need to tell us who else is in league with Satan so that I can cleanse Salem Village of evil."

Tituba began openly sobbing, finally allowing herself to give in to her fear. "If I confess, I be spared the gallows?"

"Maybe, maybe not," Parris answered, "but if you confess, you will be spared from the eternal damnation of your soul."

"But if I confess, I won't be hanged?"

"That," Parris said, "is for the court to decide. But I do believe your confession might be taken into consideration for possible leniency in your final sentence."

"That be yes?" Tituba asked. When Parris didn't answer, she

tried again, "If I confess, I be spared the gallows?"

"Your confession might help your case."

Desperation in her eyes, Tituba cried, "Yes, I be a witch!"

All of the spectators reacted violently to this incredible announcement. Some women wailed, some women swooned, and one fainted dead away. Even some men sobbed and begged God for protection. Other men shouted and banged on the benches. A few men jumped to their feet and screamed that Tituba should be hanged immediately.

But not one spectator left the courtroom.

This time the magistrate called for the outburst to cease. "I will have order in this courtroom!"

The courtroom quieted and once again the spectators sat down and became attentive, craning their necks to get a better view of the slave who had just confessed to being a witch.

"You may resume," Hathorne instructed Parris.

Parris turned to Tituba. "How did you hurt the children?"

Tituba appeared to be trying to think. "I sent a ghost at midnight to pinch them."

"What ghost?"

Tituba took a moment to answer. "The same dark spirit that Abigail saw on the rafters. The ghost from the ceiling who was pointing at Ruth."

"Who is this ghost?"

"It be Satan."

Again the spectators gasped, but before Hathorne could move to call order, the Villagers quieted down once again.

"Have you seen Satan?" Parris had an earnest look on his face, almost a maniacal expression. "What does Satan look like?"

"Wot does Satan look like?" Tituba repeated, appearing puzzled. Then she said, "Oh, yes, I see Satan. He be big, with lots of hair. Satan told me to hurt the children or else he be killing me."

"Tell me more about what Satan looks like."

"He has hair on his face. Not a beard, but hair all over. He has red eyes."

"Is he dark like you?"

"He be dark, yes."

"And so you followed Satan's orders?"

"He said he be killing me if I didn't."

Parris stroked his beard as he considered this. Suddenly he bellowed, "Who else? Who else in Salem Village follows Satan's orders? Confess!"

Tituba reared back in her chair. "You know about Goody Good and Goody Osborne."

"Who else?"

"It be no one else."

"Slave, confess!"

Tituba's eyes glistened as tears threatened once again to spill. Her gaze traveled over the courtroom, then stopped at one woman. "It be Elizabeth Proctor! She be a witch too! That's all! No others! Please, stop! No others. Please, stop."

"You swear before God in Heaven that there are no other witches in Salem Village besides Goody Good, Goody Osborne, and Mrs. Proctor?"

"I swear!"

John Proctor, the old man who had thrown water on Tituba when she had fainted, stood up from his place on the second row bench. "No!" he screamed. "My wife is a good woman! She is a good Christian, a God-fearing woman!"

Ruth was shocked at Tituba's accusation of Elizabeth Proctor, who had enough status to hold the title of Mrs. instead of Goody. She had seen Mrs. Proctor attend church every Sunday. Why would Tituba accuse a woman who was obviously devoted to the worship of the Lord God?

"Sit down," commanded the magistrate.

Seated beside her husband, Mrs. Proctor put her face in her hands and started to wail.

"No, I won't sit and take this outrage!" John Proctor stood defiantly. "My wife is a good woman. You cannot take the word of a slave over the word of a good woman. That slave is only a Negress, and an admitted witch. How can you listen to a witch's lies?"

"Sit down or you will be jailed!" Hathorne yelled.

"I don't care!" Proctor cried. "My wife is a good, God-fearing, Christian woman! She is no witch!"

Suddenly Parris turned on John Proctor and verbally attacked him. "You know you and your wife side with Israel Porter against Salem Village. You know you have helped Porter increase the taxes. And, you are the scribe who writes the contracts for the rights to waterways. You and your wife have been doing a grave disservice to Salem Village for a long, long time. You may have been doing Satan's work all along! Have you been doing the work of Satan? Are you a warlock? Have you bewitched the Villagers into giving away their hard-earned money to Salem Town?"

John Proctor threw both his hands on his chest and screamed, "I am a God-fearing man, and my wife is a God-fearing woman! I denounce this court!"

"Jail him!" yelled the magistrate. "And jail his wife!"

Suddenly from the back of the room, a handsome, middle-aged, brown-haired man stepped forward, pushing his way between the crowd until he came to the front of the courtroom. He was dressed in a starched linen shirt under a broadcloth, black woolen breeches, and blindingly white stockings.

The tall man seemed vaguely familiar to Ruth. She studied him, puzzling over where she had seen him before.

"Do you dare accuse Mrs. Proctor?" the man spoke in a calm but icy voice. He had a commanding presence. "Is it not enough that you accuse the poorest, most wretched souls of this community, that now you also seek upstanding citizens for your displays of fanaticism?"

"Do you feel that I shouldn't expose witches?" Parris stood straight and glared at the brown-haired man. "Do you side with witches? Do you make alliances with those that do evil? Israel Porter, is there something *you* wish to confess in front of the Villagers?"

Ruth had a start. Israel Porter! That's why the tall man

standing in the aisle way looked so familiar—William resembled his father.

"Parris," Israel Porter said, and Ruth felt shocked that the title of Reverend was omitted. "Parris," Porter began again, as though to emphasize the lack of title, "I side with the truth."

"You steal from the people by charging exorbitant taxes on this Village!" accused Parris.

"I am the intermediary between Salem Village and Salem Town," Porter corrected, "and currently your church accounting records do not balance. Who is doing the stealing from the Villagers? But that is a matter for a different time."

Israel Porter turned to face the old man whose wife, Elizabeth Proctor, had just been accused of witchcraft. The old man was still standing, gaping at the interaction between Porter and Parris.

"Sit down, John, before you are jailed. Don't worry, your wife will be cleared of these lies against her," Porter told Proctor. Then he faced Parris and said, "I'm announcing that there will be a protest mounted against these witchcraft proceedings, and I will take the lead in that protest."

With that, Israel Porter turned around and walked out of the courthouse.

Chapter Nine

The sun was setting, creating a visual ensemble of pinks and oranges in the western sky. Ruth trudged through the melting snow, dutifully following behind Samuel Parris, who held the hand of his niece Abigail as the trio walked home from the courthouse.

"We have to make a stop," Parris said. "We have to visit Thomas Putnam's household."

Ruth was puzzled, so she skipped briskly until she was walking alongside of Parris and Abigail. "Why are we going to my uncle's house?" she asked.

The Reverend continued to stride forward, not missing a step as he talked. "Your cousin Ann has been bewitched. She has the sickness."

"What!" Ruth cried, and stopped in her tracks. Then she raced forward to once again catch up with Parris and Abigail.

When she was back alongside of Parris, Ruth asked, "What do you mean, my cousin is sick?"

"I said that Ann Putnam is sick in bed," Parris explained as he walked, his speech visible as puffs of mist in the cold air. "Your uncle Thomas is accusing Goody Osborne of causing the sickness. That's why Goody Osborne is in jail awaiting her turn for trial."

Ruth remained directly alongside of Parris, although she had to walk quickly to keep up with his long strides. She noticed that Abigail kept up without effort, and she wondered how the twelve-year-old girl could be so physically fit if she had recently endured such physical traumas about which she had testified in court.

"Why is my Uncle Thomas accusing Goody Osborne of causing the illness?" Ruth asked, breathing hard from the brisk pace. "It could have been anyone that bewitched Ann."

Parris' voice came out as almost a growl. "Because last week, one of Goody Osborne's pigs escaped its pen and ran loose on your uncle's property. When Thomas Putnam shot the pig, Osborne cursed him. Therefore, she put a hex on his family."

"Maybe she was just upset that she lost a pig," Ruth ventured.

"She cursed your uncle," Abigail interrupted. "Now the Osborne witch's curses are coming to pass. Don't you care about your cousin, sick in bed? Where are your loyalties, anyway? You'd better not side with witches."

Greatly intimidated, Ruth became silent and slowed her pace until she once again trailed behind the Reverend and Abigail as they all trudged through the melting snow. They finally reached the Thomas Putnam household, and Ruth was surprised as a wave of nostalgia and homesickness hit her, because her uncle Thomas lived right next door to her own house.

She suddenly realized that missed her own home desperately. Ruth wished so very much for her old life, one that was without complications. She ruefully wondered how things could have remained stationary for so many years, then suddenly to have changed within a matter of two months into what her life had become now.

As they approached her uncle's house, Ruth remembered that the reason Thomas Putnam and John Putnam's houses resembled each other was because the brothers had built these two houses at roughly the same time, with one brother always helping the other. Both houses contained the same staunch ninety-degree angles as did the Parris house, because Puritans strived for function rather than form.

They knocked upon the front door, and Thomas himself answered, looking drawn and haggard from obvious lack of sleep. Like all of the Putnams, Thomas had dark blonde hair and large blue eyes. But on this day, his eyes were framed with smudges of dark pigmentation and underneath, the circles were deeply etched.

"Reverend," Thomas greeted his guest, "thank the good Lord that you are here to say prayers for my daughter. But now, my wife has taken sick too. And even Mercy Lewis is having the contortions. All are confined to their beds."

Parris, Abigail, and Ruth all stepped inside into the formal entranceway of the house. They removed their outerwear and hung them on the racks that always graced the inside of doorways.

"Your girl-servant Mercy has the illness?" Parris questioned.

Ruth knew that Mercy Lewis was the sixteen-year-old orphan who lived with and worked for Thomas Putnam. It was common for orphans to become servants to pay for their room and board. As of late, Ruth had oftentimes felt as though she herself were an orphan, even though her parents still lived. After all, didn't orphans become servants for others, just as she was for Reverend Parris?

"How is your daughter?" Parris asked as they all traveled through the house to the main staircase that would lead upstairs to the bedrooms. "Ann just turned twelve last week, didn't she?"

"Yes," Thomas confirmed, "she's twelve years old now, just like your niece. In fact, Abigail has been over here to visit Ann from time to time."

They reached the stairs, and started to climb. "Your wife, are her symptoms the same as the children?"

"The very same, but my wife's symptoms as not as severe," answered Thomas. "You'll see for yourself in a minute. Doctor Griggs is already upstairs in attendance with his bleeding bowl."

Ruth held her breath in nervous anticipation. But once she could see inside the first bedroom, Ruth relaxed, as she had been afraid that she would witness the same horrible contortions and convulsions that she had seen Betty Parris display. But there were no abhorrent displays of demonism in this room.

All of the guests entered the bedroom. There the wife, also named Ann, lay in bed, ashen-faced but quiet and still.

Parris observed the sick woman for a moment, then told

Thomas, "It appears the worst is over in this room; your wife is resting."

"Yes," Thomas said softly, "here things are under control, but now let's go into my daughter's bedroom."

The four people left the wife's room and walked across the hall. Even before the bedroom door was opened, Ruth could hear strange moaning coming from within.

When the door was finally opened, Ruth could see the interior of Ann Putnam's bedroom. It was a room without warmth or personality, just like her own room in the Parris household. But unlike her own room, this bedroom had five wooden chairs, which Ruth reasoned were provided to accommodate caregivers and well-wishers. Wooden floorboards were varnished and heavily polished and bare of rugs. The single armoire sat in the corner; a monolith that towered over the tiny bed where the afflicted child was to sleep.

But twelve-year-old Ann Putnam was not sleeping.

This was the sight that Ruth had dreaded to witness. Ann was sitting upright in her bed, having kicked all the bedlinens off. The covers and sheets lay strewn about upon the floor.

She had dark blonde hair as did Ruth herself, but Ann's hair was pulled out of her bun and fell about her face in tangled mats. The child wore a woolen nightdress as was the fashion, but it appeared torn at one shoulder. Her face glistened with sweat, and her mouth gaped open to reveal the tongue that protruded to an amazing length.

Saliva dribbled from the corners of her lips and no one moved to wipe it away so it dripped upon her lap. Her eyes were opened wide and had a fearsome appearance. Both of her arms were stretched out stiffly in front of her, appearing incapable of any flexibility. In fact, Ann's whole body seemed stiff and unyielding.

Except for the shaking.

The child quaked in convulsive spasms that were horrible to see. Periodically her head would turn towards the left and sometimes it would appear as though she was facing the wall at an impossible and unnatural angle. All though the shaking, the afflicted child's joints remained rigid, so the whole body had to move together as one single unit, the arms and legs almost as an extension of the torso and not able to move separately.

Worst of all were the sounds that Ann Putnam uttered. She moaned "uhhh, uhhh, uhhh," but from time to time bellowed a guttural sound, resembling a cow lowing in the field. It was an inhuman sound that was hideous to hear.

Doctor Griggs rose from where he had been sitting on the bed.

"She is under an evil hand," he told Parris.

"I am here to pray for her," the Reverend said, and pulled out his Bible from where he carried it under his coat.

"Please, sit down," Griggs said.

Thomas Putnam, Samuel Parris, Abigail and Ruth all sat on the wooden chairs. Doctor Griggs sat back down upon Ann's bed. All listened respectively as Parris read passages from the Bible which recounted the casting out of devils.

When the reading was finished, Parris closed the book.

"Have you arrested Goody Osborne?" Ruth's Uncle Thomas asked.

"She's been arrested," Parris acknowledged.

"She put a curse on my family," Thomas reminded everyone.

"She'll be tried in court," Parris said. Then he added, "My slave, Tituba, had her trial held earlier today. She confessed to her sins. So it was a successful trial."

Ruth felt a strong desire to interject on Tituba's behalf, but she knew she would not be allowed to speak when the adults were speaking. Actually, she was surprised that the adults were discussing political matters in front of she and Abigail at all, because usually these topics were considered inappropriate for young people to hear.

The adults continued their discussion, somehow ignoring the terrible sounds that originated from the sick child in the room.

"And Tituba exposed another witch," Parris continued.

"Who might that be?" Doctor Griggs asked.

"Elizabeth Proctor."

"Good," Thomas said, "because it's time those Proctors got their due course. Everyone knows that John Proctor is Israel Porter's ally against you, Reverend."

"Yes," Parris agreed, "I sincerely believe that John and Elizabeth Proctor had plotted against me when my back was turned. My sources tell me that John Proctor has petitioned the Village Counsel to vote me out of the parsonage."

"Not only that," Thomas Putnam added, "but John Proctor is the scribe who writes legal contracts that divide waterways, which the lawyers sign. You know as well as I do that Proctor put my farm at a disadvantage because he unfairly divided a waterway in a manner that benefited Israel Porter."

"Yes, I've heard that," Doctor Griggs joined in. "Reverend, your slave told me all about your problems with John Proctor one time when I was at your house to attend to your bedridden wife."

"Which slave?" Parris asked the doctor, "Do you mean John Indian or Tituba?"

"Why, that witch, Tituba," Doctor Griggs answered. "Of course that was before she answered to Satan's beckonings. But you know how slaves are, they listen to everything the master says. Then they don't keep it to themselves. Your Tituba knows all about your tribulations with John and Elizabeth Proctor. She told me that you were worried that Proctor will go to the Village Council in a petition against you, like you were saying just now."

The meaning of the doctor's words hit Ruth. She realized that Tituba had overheard Reverend Parris accusing John Proctor of plotting against the minister.

What better way to appease Parris other than to accuse his enemy's wife of being a witch? Wouldn't it make sense to Tituba, who was on trial for her very life, to attempt to gain favor with her accuser by pointing a finger at one of his enemies?

Could Tituba have thought that the elimination of Parris' enemy could become some sort of quid pro quo? Was that Tituba's motivation for her sudden accusal of Elizabeth Proctor of witchcraft?

Was she desperately trying to bargain with Samuel Parris for a lesser charge against herself, maybe even acquittal?

Ruth's eyes turned toward Ann Putnam, who continued to writhe in stiff, jerking spasms. Whatever afflicted Ann was very real indeed. But what about Abigail? Were her symptoms real?

Then she turned her gaze to meet that of Abigail Williams, who was staring back as though she knew exactly what Ruth was thinking. And that made Ruth afraid; very afraid.

Chapter Ten

Things changed in Salem Village.

The Villagers grew anxious; they grew paranoid, and the ones that didn't accuse their neighbors of witchcraft were afraid of being accused themselves. People mistrusted the very same friends and relatives that they had known their entire lives.

Some Villagers became so completely obsessed with spurning Satan that they eliminated anything that could have inspired joy in their lives. They felt that by acting penitent, it could bring them closer to God and could therefore protect them from witches.

Others lashed out in anger and frustration. These people were so tightly wound with nerves that they shouted at passersby to stay off their property. They stayed at home unless it was Sunday. At sundown, muskets were kept ready by the front door just in case witches came to call in the middle of the night.

Everyone was distracted. Work was neglected.

And then came the day when Giles Corey was arrested. At age 81, he was hunched and shuffling when he walked, but nonetheless he was perceived as a threat by the Villagers.

When brought to court, Giles refused to plead either innocent or guilty, and the Villagers went wild. Didn't he know that if he didn't plead, he could be tortured? That would force him to plead. Otherwise, he could get away without justice served, and the Villagers refused to allow that to happen.

Sheriff George Corwin let Giles from the dungeon-like prison to a pit in the open field next to the jail, and the old man was stripped naked, thrown to the ground, and a large board was placed on top of him. Still Giles refused to plead, so large rocks were heaved onto the board.

"What do you plead?" the sheriff bellowed.

"More weight!" Giles yelled back as he lay on the ground.

"You will pay for your obstinacy," the sheriff said. Six men lifted heavy stones, placing them one by one, on his stomach and chest. Giles' tongue fell out of his mouth with the pressure, and the sheriff simply took his cane to press it back in.

Giles Corey endured two days of the torture, and finally at noon on the second day, he died.

But instead of the town calming down after Giles' death, they became even more alarmed when an ominous sickness seemed to be rapidly spreading. A skewed portion of the population, mostly children, was afflicted with the illness characterized by convulsions and odd distortions of the limbs.

And the Villagers wondered: *Why children? Could it be because children are so innocent that they are more susceptible to witchcraft spells?*

And during all of this, four-year-old Dorcas Good wandered the street that ran in front of the jail.

The little girl had no one to look after her, and she was confused and very afraid. No one took her in, because no one wanted anything to do with the child of a witch.

Little Dorcas tried to peek into the window of the jail, not knowing that the prisoners were kept out of view. Although the prisoners were said to be housed in the jail, in reality they were chained in a dungeon underneath the main building.

Dorcas cried frequently as she wandered aimlessly about on the street. The tears created vertical lines of clean skin on her otherwise dusty face.

The little girl missed her mother. She was hungry and scared, and very alone.

Meanwhile, things were getting worse in Salem Village. The children, the poor, and some adult women continued to eat the rye bread that was contaminated with the ergot fungus.

«««—»»»

Betty Parris was preparing to leave.

She had her clothes packed in a large cloth bag, and sat on her bed, a frown on her small face. "I don't want to go," she said.

Ruth sat on Abigail's bed and made no comment. Abigail stood next to Betty's bed and told her, "You're being sent away for your own good. You'll be staying with the Sewall family in Salem Town. You know you're too young to be able to resist the witches here in the Village. You need to be someplace safe."

"Why can't you come with me?" Betty whimpered.

"Because Uncle Parris needs me," Abigail said curtly.

"Why are there witches in Salem Village, anyway?" Betty asked. She had fully recovered from her illness, but she was still pale and gaunt.

"I'm not so sure there *are* witches in Salem Village," Ruth finally spoke.

Abigail whirled to face her. "You'd better explain yourself."

Ruth felt the fear flow through her veins because she was confronting Abigail. She was well aware that this could be a very dangerous course of action. But she had not forgotten her own abandonment of Tituba during the trial, and she was still heartsick over it.

Now she had heard that the authorities had imprisoned Dorcas Good, the four-year-old daughter of the beggarwoman, simply because the Village elders had nowhere else to put the child. Elizabeth Proctor had also been jailed and now the old man who had tried to defend her in court, John Proctor, was being accused. And there were others.

When would it end? Ruth felt she just couldn't continue to go along with the incredible insanity that seemed to be all around her. She decided that if she couldn't stop it, then at least she wouldn't participate in it.

"I'm not saying anything." She tried to remain calm. "I'm thinking that perhaps there's a real reason why people are getting sick. Maybe this illness is something like the consumption or smallpox. Except maybe this particular sickness is something we aren't sure about. God is perfect, but is his creation? People are like a vessel; the inside is good but on the outside, the body can be broken. Maybe that's all it is—maybe there's nothing more to it than that. You were probably just sick, and it may have affected your judgment."

"My judgment? I think you're calling me a liar," Abigail said, and Ruth felt chills of apprehension.

"I didn't hear Ruth call you a liar," Betty said.

Abigail whirled around again, this time to threaten Betty. "You'd better remember that Tituba taught me witchcraft spells! I haven't forgotten how to cast them. I could cast a spell on you."

Betty gasped. "If you can cast spells, then how do I know *you're* not a witch?"

"Tituba taught me the spells, not Satan," Abigail sniffed. "That's the difference. Satan is the one who taught Tituba."

"I don't think Tituba taught you any spells." As she said it, Ruth was wondering how she could be so brave as to express her thoughts out loud, but she couldn't seem to stop herself.

Abigail faced Ruth. "Maybe Tituba did teach me spells and maybe she didn't. But you're not sure, are you? Anyway, what you really ought to think about," she said, narrowing her small dark eyes, "is that if you side against me, you'll be sorry. After all, I have your missing button. I could tell my uncle where I found it. Is that what you want?"

Betty asked what button, but the other girls ignored her.

"You'd better not side against me."

Suddenly Abigail once again became the chameleon, because she brightened visibly. "It's time for dinner, and this is Betty's last meal in this house for awhile. Let's all go downstairs."

But when the trio reached the bottom of the main staircase, Reverend Parris was waiting at the foot of the steps. "You," he pointed at Ruth, "go into the kitchen and help John Indian serve the meal. Since Tituba has consorted with the Devil, she is paying her penitence in jail until she hangs and goes to Hell. But that means that you must take her place to do Tituba's duties in this household."

Having no recourse, Ruth went to the kitchen. John Indian

was ladling soup from a kettle into a large serving bowl, unusual in its design because it had two handles on the sides.

"This be the first course," he commented.

Ruth looked at him. "John," she ventured, "how are you feeling?"

He stopped and examined the large bowl in his hands. It was white, and unadorned with any design except for the potter's initials on the bottom. "I be feeling better."

"John," Ruth wanted to know, "I heard you accused your wife of being a witch. Why?"

"Better to accuse," he said slowly, "than to be accused."

John handed Ruth the serving bowl, then added, "Right before you came here, Tituba had a baby."

Ruth stared at him in amazement. "I've never seen a baby. Where's the baby?"

"Out back."

Ruth strained to look out the kitchen window. She saw nothing but the barn in the distance. "Where out back?"

"In the ground," John said and Ruth felt her arms prickle with goosebumps. "That baby be born dead."

"Oh!" Ruth exclaimed. "I'm sorry."

John told her, "Don't be sorry. That baby was not meant to be. You see, that baby be born white."

Ruth was so stunned that she almost dropped the soup she was holding. She could feel the blood drain from her face. Still, she turned around and walked out of the kitchen. She felt dazed, but she still managed to maintain her composure long enough to place the large bowl of soup on the dining room table. She began serving the soup, willing her hands not to shake.

She felt immense shock. A mulatto baby! She recalled what John Indian had told her a previous time in that same kitchen.

"They are sins of the father," John had said.

At the time he had uttered those words, Ruth had had no idea what John was talking about. But now it hit her and she understood the implications: that the father of Tituba's child had been white.

But had it been Tituba's choice to have had relations with a white man? John said it was the sins of the father. Could a white man have forced himself upon her? Who was the child's father? Could that white man have been. . .she turned to look at Reverend Parris, who ignored her. No, it wasn't possible. Was it?

After she placed the soup on the table, Ruth went back into the kitchen. She didn't ask John any more questions, but mechanically continued to go back and forth until all of the food was placed upon the dining room table.

Ruth's mind was reeling. She would never really know who fathered Tituba's mulatto baby. But now she knew what her husband held against her, and why he acted so coldly towards his wife.

Finally both she and John Indian sat at the table with the small Parris family. As usual, Mrs. Parris was absent, so sick that she remained upstairs. But after all this time, no one missed Mrs. Parris or even thought about her. Reverend Parris was a man who had not shared his wife's company for a long, long time, much less his wife's bed.

Samuel Parris lifted the Bible and began to read. "For there is nothing covered, that shall not be revealed; neither hid, that shall not be known. But I will forewarn you whom ye shall fear. Fear him which after he hath killed hath power to cast into Hell; yea, I say unto you, fear him."

Parris lifted his head, "That's in Saint Luke. The 'fear him' means to fear Satan. Satan will not be covered nor hid, because I will personally reveal his evil. I will personally eliminate Satan's influences from Salem Village."

After grace, Ruth continued to keep her eyes downcast. Numbly she ate her meal. She was so quiet that suddenly Parris questioned her.

"What grieves you?" he asked. "I'm concerned. You aren't getting sick, are you?"

Ruth couldn't bring herself to look at him. "I don't think so."

"I care about you," Parris said, "because blessed be the servant. Besides, you are doing very well here in my household. I think I'd like you to stay for a while. I can arrange it with your father."

Ruth could feel Abigail stiffen beside her. An alarm went off in Ruth's mind. She sensed Abigail's anger.

And Abigail had ways to make people who angered her disappear from this household.

Abigail had seen to it that Tituba was gone. Now Ruth wondered if Abigail had engineered Betty's pending departure, too. Wouldn't Abigail feel threatened with Parris's love for his daughter? Wouldn't getting rid of Betty be another step into maneuvering a situation where Abigail could have her uncle in this house all to herself?

If Abigail had indeed maneuvered the departure of her cousin Betty, then that left Ruth as the only other female in this house that Abigail might view as competition for her uncle's affection.

Abigail was obsessed with her uncle. And her uncle had just expressed a caring for Ruth.

That meant Ruth was in dangerous territory.

"I'm fine," Ruth said hastily to Parris. "I'm just tired."

But after the meal, when Ruth was alone in the kitchen washing the dishes in the big sink, Parris entered. She was nervously aware of the Reverend's presence as he stood beside her.

He stood close, so close.

"Aren't I washing the dishes correctly?" Ruth could think of nothing else to say, but the silence between them had unsettled her tremendously so she wanted to break it.

"As the master of this household," Parris said softly, "the servants are to do my bidding."

"I've done everything you've told me," Ruth tried to step backwards; to put some distance between them, no matter how small.

"A man of God lives in two worlds," Parris said, "the spiritual and the natural. To be able to fulfill my duties as a spiritual leader, there is the wellbeing of my flesh to consider. I need to be healthy in my body in order to have the strength in my mind to lead the Villagers through this time of great evil. You would be doing God's work if you assisted me in my efforts."

Ruth didn't like the sound of any of this. "What am I supposed to do?"

"Ruth," Parris stepped next to her again, "you are no longer a child—you are becoming a woman. Women are placed upon the earth to serve men. Eve was created by our Lord God for the sole purpose of becoming a companion to Adam. The Bible dictates that a woman should cleave unto a man."

"I don't know what you mean." She heard her voice shake.

"Ruth," Parris leaned so close to her that she could smell his breath, "you trust me to know what is good for you, right? You were put into this household by your father in order to learn the skills to be marketable as a wife. You trust your father's judgment of me as your teacher, do you not?"

Suddenly both Ruth and Parris were startled by the loud crashing sound of a dish dropping onto the kitchen floor. They whirled around, and discovered that Abigail Williams was standing in front of the kitchen door, a small plate broken at her feet.

"How long have you been there, spying on me?" Parris asked.

"Long enough," Abigail said. The she turned and went out the door, leaving the shards of china pottery still lying on the floor.

Reverend Parris said nothing, but he left Ruth's side and walked out of the kitchen to follow his niece. Ruth stood staring after him for a moment, then went over to the doorway. She kneeled down to begin picking up the shards of broken pottery.

Ruth didn't want to think about what had just happened. Instead, Ruth wondered if things would ever begin to seem normal in the bizarre house where she now lived.

But if she thought the worst had happened, she was unprepared for the horror of events to follow.

Early the next morning, Doctor Griggs was summoned to the Parris household. Reverend Parris rode to fetch the doctor himself, because John Indian was busy delivering Betty to the Stephen Sewall residence in Salem Town and therefore was unavailable.

That morning, Ruth wasn't sure what was going on, but she understood that Abigail was having some sort of seizures. Abigail was in her bedroom, but Ruth was back in the kitchen again. She boiled water in a huge kettle in the cooking fireplace, preparing to wash clothes. She had made the soap the day before.

But soon the front door banged open and Parris burst inside, closely followed by Doctor Griggs. Startled, Ruth came into the parlor to meet them.

The men were just about to stride to the main staircase, when they both stopped in their tracks.

Abigail was coming down the stairs.

Still in her woolen nightdress, Abigail began running, taking the stairs two steps at a time. Her eyes were wide and her expression was one of terror.

About half way into her descent, she suddenly threw her arms up in the air and cried "Whoosh! Whoosh!" as she reached the bottom of the staircase. She didn't stop there, but reached a full gallop, and ran right past the startled men who stood gaping at her in disbelief. Abigail raced into the kitchen.

Both Parris and Griggs quickly recovered from their astonishment and followed Abigail. Ruth trailed after them, too curious to stay behind.

Abigail ran right for the cooking stove, and with her bare hands, she began to grab coals and fling them every which way. For a moment Parris and Griggs were too surprised to move, but then Doctor Griggs snapped out of his immobility and rushed to stop the twelve-year-old girl who was acting deranged.

Griggs grabbed Abigail and pinned her arms to her side. He held her in a bear hug until she cried, "Let me go! Let me go!"

Reluctantly, Griggs released his grip.

Instantly Abigail dropped to the floor, writhing as if in pain. She twisted and thrashed about on the wooden floor like some sort of horribly wounded animal. She gnashed her teeth and snapped at the air, then alternately snarled like a dog and squealed like a pig.

Horrified, Ruth ran to Abigail and tried to help the girl sit up. But any attempts Ruth made to touch Abigail only resulted in more frenzied displays of bizarre twistings of her torso and archings of her back as she rolled on the floor.

"Get Ruth away from me!" Abigail screamed.

"What?" Ruth took a step backwards.

"Uncle Parris!" Abigail cried. "Uncle Parris!"

"I'm here," Parris came forward.

"Uncle Parris, save me!" And suddenly, Abigail sprang to her feet and threw herself into her uncle's arms.

He held his niece, and Abigail sobbed into his shirt. "Dear child, what's ailing you?" Parris cried. "Who is tormenting you?"

"It's an evil spirit that's possessing her," declared Doctor Griggs. "Abigail is under an evil hand."

"Yes!" Abigail finally let go of her uncle and stepped away from him. "I'm being bewitched. I'm being tormented. All night I was bitten and pinched. I wanted to come out and tell you, Uncle Parris, I really did, but I was so afraid! I couldn't come out of my room, because there was a witch stopping me from getting out of my bed."

"Who was it?" Parris demanded. "What evil spirit haunted you in the middle of the night? Was it the specter of one of the jailed witches? Did one of the prisoners send an apparition? Or is there yet another witch that remains free? Who torments you, child?"

Abigail raised her hand, and her finger pointed directly at Ruth. "That one!" she cried. "It's Ruth Putnam! It is a dreadful thing to have a devil in the house of a man of God. Stop Ruth. She is a witch!"

And at that, Abigail collapsed upon the floor in a faint.

Doctor Griggs bent over and gently picked Abigail up in his arms. "I'll put this poor afflicted child into her bed," he informed Parris.

Then Griggs looked at Ruth, but spoke to Parris. "Reverend, you'd better take this evil witch to the magistrate."

Chapter Eleven

Ruth opened her eyes.

She had, for the brief period she was able to sleep, forgotten where she was. But now she came fully awake, and the horror of her situation assaulted all of her five senses.

She felt the manacles upon her wrists, binding them together. She could at least take some comfort that she was not chained to the wall; instead, her wrists were bound in front of her. She knew there were only three wall manacles in the Salem Village dungeon underneath the jail, and those three were already occupied by other accused witches.

The sounds in the dungeon were many. In the far corner, four-year-old Dorcas leaned against her mother, Sarah Good, who was one of those chained against the wall. Ruth could hear the child whimpering, and she knew that although Dorcas wanted to cling to her mother, she was unable because the child's wrists were chained as was everyone's.

Little Dorcas could only lean against her mother, desperately seeking some sort of physical contact for comfort. The small child was only one of those in the dungeon who was softly crying and moaning.

Ruth heard scratching sounds, and wondered if rats had found their way into the dark dungeon.

Other sounds permeated. Because the jail was located within a mile of the river, she knew that it was sunk into a water table, hence the dripping. She knew that water found its way into cracks into the dungeon masonry and she could hear its leaking. Because of the seeping water, the floor was damp and cold as ice; it was only the middle of March so winter was still upon Massachusetts.

Ruth was crouched in the middle of the cellar to avoid the wet walls, and she had sympathy for the first three women accused of witchcraft, because those three were shackled to the sides of the dungeon. Those three could not move away from the water that dripped freely and ran down the sides of the cellar in small rivulets.

The three women who were chained against the wall were Tituba Indian, Sarah Good, and Sarah Osborne.

The smells in the dungeon were terrible. Fungus smells and the scent of things rotting from the water mingled with other repugnant odors, such as unwashed bodies and human feces. But Ruth found herself surprised that her nose was actually getting used to these dreadful smells, and that after her first hour in this place, her sense of smell had somehow adjusted to an extent that her eyes no longer watered from inhaling the stench.

Even her sense of taste was affected. Because of the immense fear she had felt when she had been brought in early yesterday morning, now her mouth had a copper taste and she wanted a drink of water so intensely that it was yet another thing to add to her misery.

A horizontal opening, about three feet long and six inches wide, was a sort of window in the cellar, located up at the level of the ceiling. There was no glass upon it, and it was bare of any screening. This small opening allowed some sun to stream into the dismal dungeon. The window was above ground level, and it was the only source of light.

Ruth looked at that opening, and despite the fact that it let more cold into the room, she was grateful for the fresh air that it allowed inside. She mused that in summer, the number of flies and other biting insects that window would invite probably made for some intense suffering of a different nature than what the inhabitants had to bear now.

She looked around. She could see how many people were imprisoned with her. How had this happened? How could all these people, including herself, be doomed to the basement jail?

When she had been thrown down in this cave-like dungeon

the previous morning, she was so terrified that she personalized her situation and didn't care about the other people occupying the same space. But now she was surprised at how many people were in this prison. And she recognized most of them.

Ruth saw Rebecca Nurse, an older woman who had years earlier been involved in a land dispute with the Putnams. For a moment, Ruth wondered if her own father had had any hand in Rebecca's arrest; but instantly dismissed the idea.

She saw Mary Easty, the sister of Rebecca Nurse. She realized that relatives of accused witches could also be subject to suspicion themselves.

She saw Martha Cory, another Salem Village outcast who at one time had given birth to an illegitimate son. Even though she had eventually married Giles Cory and now was a middle-aged woman, the taint still followed Martha. Ruth knew that Martha's husband Giles was much older than she and was considered to be a cantankerous character about the Village.

Ruth had known that Elizabeth Proctor would be inhabiting this terrible prison, but she was surprised to see Elizabeth's husband, John Proctor, down here also. Her heart went out to the couple as she saw that they were huddled together, both crouched upon the damp earthen floor of the dungeon. Ruth observed that John was attempting to soothe his wife, a much younger woman than he; and his love for her was obvious.

But there were others in the underground prison that Ruth didn't recognize. She wondered, *How can all these people be witches? How could this terrible thing have escalated to such an extent that all these people are jailed? For that matter, how could the accusations of witchcraft have even begun in the first place?*

And then she thought: *How did I get in here? I am no witch.*

Ruth listened to the rantings of Sarah Good, who seemed out of her head. Little Dorcas was now crouched on the ground, resting on her haunches, and rocking back and forth with her head buried in her manacled hands.

She heard the moanings of Sarah Osborne, who appeared very sick and who was drooped down; being held up only by the manacles that were bolted into the wall. She heard the murmurings of John Proctor as he attempted to comfort his beloved Elizabeth. She listened to a young woman that she did not recognize, who was quietly beseeching God for deliverance out of this terrible nightmare.

Ruth was cold; so very cold. Her fingers were icy and her nose was running freely. She wore a cloak over her heavy dress; still, the winter chill penetrated her clothes and she could feel the cold damp air in her very being.

She found her thoughts drifting as she tried to cope with the traumatism of her situation.

She tried to find some sort of perspective on the events happening around her. She searched her memory for any psalms or parables that preached strength, but her mind came up blank. She looked into her soul to find her faith.

Would she be able to maintain her sanity through the fear and the abhorrence, through the shock and the depression, and through every other inconsolable emotion she experienced from finding herself chained in a dungeon? Ruth realized that soon she could very well be put to death. How could God allow this to happen?

Ruth decided that it was not God who would soon sentence her to hang, but the lawmakers of Salem Village. She contemplated that having faith meant having trust in God, and having trust lessened her stress. It gave her a sense that, in a world that seemed out of order, someone or something was still good and caring. If she had to die, then having faith made her feel that it would not be the end of everything. Life would not go on as she had known it, but it would somehow go on.

So that was the design of faith, Ruth mused. It could keep her sane when the world around her was insane.

But as she huddled on the cold, damp, earthen floor of the dungeon, suddenly the trap door at the top of the wooden steps opened.

Ruth blinked in the unexpected light. Someone was entering the cellar.

All at once, most of the prisoners began crying out, begging for release. They pleaded with whoever was descending the steps. As the light shone behind the man's back, nobody could tell who was entering the dungeon because he appeared only as a dark figure coming down the stairs.

When the man reached the bottom, he said, "I have come for Bridget Bishop and Ruth Putnam. Identify yourselves."

A sweet, strong voice called, "I'm here."

Ruth looked to see who was speaking, and discovered it was the young woman who had been praying to God for deliverance just moments ago. In the dim light of the dungeon, Ruth thought that Bridget didn't appear to be much older than herself, perhaps twenty at the most.

Not knowing what else to do, Ruth followed suit and also called, "I'm here."

"Both of you, get up," the man said, and Ruth didn't recognize the voice. "Follow me."

"Why?" asked Ruth. "Where are you taking us?"

The man stopped and looked at her. "You'd rather stay here in this filth? Insolent witch, aren't you? You're lucky I don't strip you naked and search your body for hidden teats upon which you nurse your familiars. But you're wanted upstairs. Hathorne is about to hold your trial."

"Don't talk to him," Bridget advised from alongside. Grateful that she wasn't going through this alone, Ruth managed a weak smile towards Bridget.

They climbed the steep steps, which were only wooden boards. Ruth was surprised that the boards had not already rotted from the damp, and sighed in relief when they all made it to the top.

She soon found herself back in the courtroom. Again there was an overflow of people, as the room's seating capacity had been more than exceeded. Again almost everyone from the Village was in attendance, all craning their necks for a better view of the morbid proceedings.

She looked at her surroundings. The Village hall was small,

and the unyielding wooden pews were jammed with spectators, and in front of the seating area was a dark wooden railing, almost as though to hold people back. Just as before, there was no jury. There was a wooden platform in front, and upon it was the box for the magistrate to sit and reign over the courtroom.

Except this time, Ruth was seeing the courtroom from a different perspective. Directly alongside the magistrate's chair was the witness chair. But this time, instead of Tituba, the witness chair was where *she* now sat. This time, she was not among the Villagers as a mere spectator.

Instead, she was the reason everyone had come. This time, Ruth was the main event.

Ruth looked at where Bridget Bishop sat in the front of the room in a corner. She tried to catch Bridget's eye, but the young woman had her head down and her eyes downcast.

Both Bridget and Ruth still had their wrists chained. Earlier, Ruth had suffered intense cold in the dungeon. But now, in the crowded courtroom, she discovered that the cloak she still wore over her winter dress created the opposite effect. Here in the courtroom, warmed by so many bodies, she felt uncomfortably hot, and the sweat occasionally trickled down from her brow, entering and stinging her eyes with salt. But she was unable to rub her eyes because the shackles that bound her wrists prevented any efforts to allow herself some relief. She could not even wipe her own face.

"Hear ye," John Hathorne bellowed, and the courtroom came to order. "This is a trial where the accusers shall give witness. The accusers are Abigail Williams, Mary Walcott, Elizabeth Hubbard, Mercy Lewis, and Ann Putnam."

Ruth couldn't suppress a gasp. Ann Putnam! Her own cousin was accusing her of witchcraft!

And, how had the list of accusers swelled from just Abigail and Mary to now five young girls?

Hathorne continued, "Two persons are hereby accused of witchcraft. The two persons are Ruth Putnam and Bridget Bishop. These two accused will have to prove their innocence or else they will be judged as guilty. Conviction means death by hanging. Reverend Parris, you may question the accused."

But before Parris could rise and walk to the front of the courtroom, there was a small commotion within the crowd. Waves of people parted to allow someone to approach from the rear of the room. A handsome, middle-aged, brown-haired man stepped forward, pushing his way through the crowd.

Ruth recognized the man instantly as the same man who had made his public protest against the witchcraft proceedings before in this very same courtroom.

Israel Porter stood at the railing which separated the crowd from the court officials. His mere presence inspired awe in Ruth because he seemed so confident in his demeanor that he projected a sort of omnipotence.

"Where are the lawyers?" Porter asked.

Parris' face reddened and he went up to the front of the courtroom, standing in front of the magistrate's bench. It was as though Parris wanted to silently signal to the crowd that he, by standing next to Hathorne, shared the power of the court officials. Then he turned to face Israel Porter.

"No lawyer is necessary," Parris said loudly enough for all to hear. "If these women accused of witchcraft are innocent, then the good Lord God will see that they are delivered from conviction. God will only allow sinners to hang."

"But," Porter said calmly, "although God is indeed perfect, these trials are not held by God. These trials are held by men, who are imperfect. The good Lord cannot instill common sense in men who were unfortunate enough to be born without."

The courtroom instantly erupted in pandemonium at Israel Porter's public display of insolence. How dare he insinuate that officials of the court have no common sense?

"Israel Porter, you are on dangerous ground," warned Hathorne.

"Now, now, let's all retain our composure and look at this situation with logic." Porter's calm was contagious; people settled back onto their benches. Everyone wanted to hear what this inconceivable man would say next.

"You are interrupting this courtroom!" cried Parris. He turned to the magistrate. "Your Honor, evict this man."

"Let's wait and hear what Porter has to say," Hathorne said, surprising Parris with this sudden change of allegiance.

Suddenly Parris understood. Israel Porter was the intermediary between Salem Town and Salem Village. And the taxes collected by Porter paid the salary of John Hathorne. Politically, Israel Porter was a very important man.

"What do you suggest?" Hathorne asked Porter.

Israel Porter wore neatly pressed black broadcloth and breeches, and the blindingly white stockings. His whole appearance was striking, and he was a man to be noticed.

"I suggest," he told the courtroom, "that there be a test for Ruth Putnam. This way, real evidence can be obtained, and it would be tangible evidence as to whether she is a witch or not. Take her outside, and throw her into the river. If Ruth Putnam saves herself through sorcery, then we will all know beyond a doubt that she is a witch."

"I say we continue with the court proceedings as was originally intended," Parris offered, anger in his voice at being undermined.

"Why?" Porter looked at Parris. "So that you can continue to parade your feelings of self-importance before all the Villagers?"

If it was red before, Parris' face now turned purple. "I protest your rudeness!"

"And I protest these court proceedings," Porter countered.

"We'll have order in this courtroom," Hathorne said without conviction. He turned to Porter. "Your idea is a good one. When shall we take Miss Putnam to the river?"

"How about right now?" Porter suggested. "In fact, I have arranged a horse to be outside at this very moment. The horse is all saddled and ready for the accused. I have an escort to guide the horse. So right now is a very good time; a very good time indeed."

"Bring the accused outside," Hathorne ordered, and the man

who had retrieved Ruth from the dungeon sprang into action. Roughly he grabbed Ruth by the arms and jerked her off the witness chair to her feet. The man got behind her and pushed her through the crowd towards the door. They followed Porter, who led the way.

They exited the courtroom and entered the street, and Ruth blinked in the sunlight that held the promise of spring. She was pushed towards a waiting horse, tied to another horse upon which a man sat, wearing the traditional Puritan hat. However, this man's hat was pulled excessively low over his face, so that his features were obscured in a shadow.

The jailer who had retrieved Ruth from the dungeon pushed Ruth up on the horse. She tried to balance herself, because she could not use her shackled hands to grab the reins.

Israel Porter went over to her with a rope and tied her securely in the saddle. His gentleness surprised her. "Be calm," he said softly.

The crowd was exiting the courtroom and milling about in the street. Nobody wanted to miss a moment of the witch being sent to the water test.

Suddenly, Ruth felt her horse bolt forward. She panicked and became terrified that she would fall off her horse. But the rope prevented her fall by securing her onto the saddle.

She felt her fear escalate as her horse began to gallop. She could hear the crowd behind her collectively cry out in anger and dismay, but she was powerless to stop her horse, which seemed to be running out of control.

Then she became was aware that she was not alone. Right next to her was the escort on the other horse, galloping at her side. Ruth realized that the escort was actually leading her horse with a rope tied to his own.

The hat that had shadowed the escort's features fell off in the wind.

Ruth looked into the face of William Porter, who was taking her on a mad dash for freedom.

Chapter Twelve

They rode very fast for what seemed to be a long distance.

Eventually William reined his horse to a stop at a dense grove of trees when they reached the outskirts of the Salem Village boundary. Although the deciduous trees had not yet leafed out, there were many evergreens to shelter them from prying eyes.

Ruth's horse stopped as well. Unable to dismount because of the shackles still upon her wrists, she waited for William to climb off his horse and approach her.

He stood by her mount and asked, "Ready to take off your bracelets?"

She looked down at him from her position high up on the saddle. "How? They're locked."

"I have a key." William grinned. "It's called bribery."

"You bribed a jailer?" Ruth was dumbfounded.

"Of course," he told her as he unlocked the manacles.

Ruth rubbed her wrists and silently rejoiced at her sudden and unexpected freedom. She remained on her horse as William began untying the rope that secured her to the saddle.

But then both she and William heard the sounds of hoofbeats rapidly approaching. "Over here!" called an unknown voice from not too far away. "I see them!"

Frightened, Ruth exclaimed, "What shall we do?"

"We ride!" With that, William bolted for his horse, and threw himself upon the saddle. "Follow me!" he cried to Ruth.

She shook the reins with all her might and aimed her horse at the haunches of the mount in front of her. Spirited, her horse instantly obeyed and jumped into a mad gallop. Ruth was unused to straddling the saddle like a man, but found that her legs around each side of the horse's ribs helped to steady her as the animal raced ahead.

Ruth snapped again at the reins, and her horse practically leaped, but she managed to hold on. Her dress hampered the grip her legs had around her mount.

Suddenly, she heard a *whoosh* right by her ear. She realized with horror that the sound must have been a musket ball. Someone was shooting at her! If she hadn't moved her horse at that very second, the passing ball would have found its mark right into her flesh.

She could hear hoofbeats thundering behind her as their trackers followed in pursuit. To avoid any more musket balls, she tried to stagger the direction in which her horse ran, but the animal resisted anything except a straightforward course.

Ruth desperately tried to keep her horse following William's mount. But then William turned his horse off the road and into the weeds and underbrush of terrain that was unknown to her. She pushed her horse forward, trying to evade the trees and praying that her mount could avoid any animal holes on the ground.

But her luck didn't hold, because suddenly a deer burst from the underbrush directly into Ruth's path. Her horse was startled, and it stopped too abruptly for her to compensate. The horse reared up in a frightened reaction to the deer and she felt herself sliding backwards over the mount's hindquarters. Desperately grabbing for the saddle in an attempt to pull herself back to a position of control, Ruth missed and as her horse bolted forward, she felt herself free-fall for seemingly endless moments until she hit the hardpan of the ground.

Her horse ran off without her, leaving her lying on the ground.

Winded, she gasped for breath but it was knocked out of her. She felt lightning bolts of pain shoot from her right elbow as she had used that arm in an attempt to break her fall. She felt emotionally sick as she realized she was helpless to move without having the time to recover from the blow of the fall. And she could hear a horse approaching rapidly.

But suddenly William was directly above her, and his horse was stomping its feet so close to her that she thought she would be trampled. William leaned down from his saddle and reached for her.

She threw both her arms up, hoping that he would be able to grasp at least one of her hands. He did grab her hand and yanked so hard that he literally lifted her off the ground. Pulling her on his horse behind himself, William urged the animal to once more bolt forward into a gallop, and he snapped the reins again and again.

"They've got muskets!" Ruth yelled in his ear. She had her arms gripped tightly around William's chest, but there was no time to consider Puritan decency. She was just so very, very grateful that he was there.

"Don't worry! This is the fastest horse in all the Village!" William yelled back, but in the passing wind his voice sounded faint and distant.

He continued the course he had chosen that led through the underbrush, and Ruth buried her face into his back as she gripped him tightly. She locked her fingers together over his chest so she wouldn't fall. The horse seemed confident and didn't shy from the rough terrain. The snow was all but melted, yet there were slippery spots and she prayed to God that the mount wouldn't slide. The animal seemed sure-footed, and when she no longer heard the pursuing hoofbeats behind her, Ruth began to feel elated.

Perhaps they would escape after all.

Perhaps.

It was almost too much to hope for.

But she realized that they must have outrun their pursuers, because she could feel William's arms pulling back on the reins, slowing the horse to a canter.

She couldn't believe that she was still alive.

"I'm taking you to a secret place," William called back to her as his horse continued its canter. "You'll be all right there."

"Why are you doing this for me?" Of all the things she could have said, she didn't know why that came out of her mouth.

He laughed. "Because I want to marry you. I couldn't very well do that if you were hanged, now, could I?"

She didn't believe him, but giddy with relief that she still had her life, Ruth laughed. She was happy, and it was enough for now. She wanted to know where he was taking her, but she decided not to ask any more questions. She would just wait and see.

Chapter Thirteen

Ruth sat on the back haunches of the horse, moving her hips in time to the animal's gait. William had slowed the horse to a walk, and the couple headed east, past the little village of Ipswich.

They rode in silence, but Ruth heard birds singing. She felt the sweat of the horse beneath her after its hard ride. The day was crisp and clear and the air smelled like damp earth as the snow melted into the ground. Because Ruth was aware that she had narrowly escaped death, she was newly appreciative of the world around her. Suddenly things that she had once taken for granted held new meaning.

She had never been out of Salem Village in her entire life. What she was doing right now was more adventure than she could ever have imagined for herself even a month ago. The very idea that she was sitting close to a man who was not her husband, with her arms around him, would have been at one time too scandalous to even consider. But thinking that way was something she had done in another life; a different life.

Today was a brand new day, and she was a brand new person.

She had come so close to being sentenced to hang for witchcraft. Now she felt that God was giving her a second chance. Because of this, she would live a new life, and she would live it differently.

She resolved that she would no longer be the timid mouse she had always been. Now she knew she would view people's motivations with a bit more skepticism. She made a pact with herself that, in the future, she would not be so trusting in other people's opinions unless it made sense to her. She decided that, from now on, she would be braver and more vocal in her own opinions whenever she saw injustices. Perhaps she could make a difference in outcomes.

In this second chance, Ruth felt she would embrace life to the fullest. She would take less for granted and she would allow herself to feel some happiness if opportunities were presented to her.

She finally understood how fragile life could be and how quickly it could be taken away. She didn't want to waste a minute of her life anymore; she wanted to live it to the fullest.

She had seen so much horror in the last few months. She felt so much older because of it. Ruth thought about it—what Reverend Parris had said that day in the kitchen was true. He had said that she was no longer a child. But she had become a woman in different ways than what Parris had meant.

Now Ruth sensed she was stronger and more capable. She had been through so much and had managed to survive without losing her mind or her spirit. She realized now that she had more resilience than she had ever known she possessed.

She considered William. Would he be part of her future? She found the idea tantalizing. As she rode behind him, she daydreamed. Surely he was joking when he told her he wanted to marry her. But…could it be possible? Could it?

When they got to wherever they were going, would he try to kiss her again? And if he did, this time, would she let him?

She was very conscious that her arms were wrapped around him. Was William thinking about that, too?

They continued to ride without speaking. They went through country that contained no homes or buildings of any sort, but eventually they came to a barn that appeared to be sitting all by itself in a vast field. Surrounding the barn, the grass was still brown from being covered by the now melting winter blanket of snow, and tree branches were just beginning to swell with new buds.

William reined in his horse. "We're stopping here."

Ruth grinned. "Where is 'here?'"

He dismounted carefully so he wouldn't jostle her. Then he

stood on the ground and pointed to a grove of trees. "Beyond those trees is a house. We'll put the horse in a stall and then walk the rest of the way. This property belongs to Daniel Green. He owns over four hundred acres, so his house is very secluded. Daniel's son Joseph is visiting right now. Joseph has just graduated from University and is being ordained as a minister."

When William reached for Ruth to help her out of her saddle, he noticed her frown. "Don't worry," he said quickly, "Joseph Green is different. You'll see."

Ruth stood next to the horse, and said, "Reverend Parris is the only minister I know, because I don't remember Reverend Lawson very well. Deodat Lawson was the minister in Salem Village before Reverend Parris."

"I know," William smiled at her, and she was charmed. "The high powers in Salem Village drove Lawson off."

"You're very aware of political things, aren't you?" she asked.

He laughed. "You should be glad I care about politics," he told her. "You got rescued because of it. Your rescue made a statement to the magistrate that not all of the Villagers are going to just sit back and watch him hang innocent people. You see, you were not only the victim of bad judgment but also of bad politics. The political system is insane if it allows innocent people to be snatched off the street and thrown in dungeons."

He hesitated, then continued, "I'm part of a small group of Villagers who want to put a stop to the oppressive and prejudicial government that is currently running Salem Village. This small group of people holds meetings where plans are made. So, because I'm the politically-minded sort that I am, you weren't hanged."

She asked, "Is that the only reason you rescued me? To make a political statement?"

He stopped and looked at her, his handsome face serious. "Here's the real reason: I rescued you because from the very first time I met you, I knew you were special. I care about you. I care about you a lot."

Then he started leading the horse into the barn. "Besides," he added with a mischievous grin, "you're much too pretty to hang."

Ruth stood outside in the sunlight for a moment, too surprised at his words to follow. She watched him disappear into the gloom of the barn. Then she realized that her mouth was open and so she shut it, thinking that she must look like a fool, gaping and staring the way she was.

But she was elated. He made her feel like she had never felt before. It was as though being with him actually triggered physical changes within herself: her heart beat irregularly, her breath became short, and her hands shook.

She wondered—was this love?

How could she tell? She had no experience from which to draw upon, so she realized that she was very naïve, even as to her own feelings.

Jerking herself into motion, Ruth followed William into the gloom of the barn. She was grateful, no matter what his reasons were, that he had rescued her at great personal risk to himself. She found herself wondering how he had managed the getaway.

"I want to thank you for what you did for me," she told him.

He smiled but didn't reply.

"What about your father?" she asked. "Did Israel Porter know you were outside of the courthouse, waiting for me?"

William had put the horse in a stall, surrounded by sweet-smelling hay and straw. He began unhooking the bridle. "My father not only knew, but he planned the whole thing."

Ruth digested that. Then she wondered, "Won't your father be arrested for conspiracy?"

"Hathorne doesn't have that kind of power," William explained as he unsaddled the horse. "Hathorne may be a member of the provincial legislature of Salem Village, but my father once held office in the General Court with Sir William Phipps, who's now the governor of Massachusetts. So, my father is more powerful than Hathorne because he has more influence. These days my father serves as a selectman in Salem Town. That's why he is the intermediary between the Village and the

Town."

William picked up a cloth and began rubbing down the horse's flanks. "As for what's going on in Salem Village," he continued, changing the subject, "at one time, the so-called 'bewitched' children were only accusing persons of witchcraft who were the downtrodden of Salem Village. The accused were social outcasts, and those poor misfits had no method with which to fight back against the accusers, or the courts, for that matter."

He added, "But now, the children are accusing upright citizens of witchcraft. Now they point fingers at pious Christians."

"Why?"

"Well," William said as he rubbed the horse with the cloth, "it is quite possible that, lately, someone is suggesting a list of people to those bewitched children."

Ruth was stunned. "Why on earth would someone do that?"

William grinned ruefully. "To eliminate enemies."

"But," Ruth couldn't believe what she was hearing, "nobody would go that far to get rid of someone they didn't like."

"Like or dislike has nothing to do with it," William told her. "John Proctor writes the deeds to waterways, and he is in jail. Mary Easty and her husband have the rights to who can cut trees in the woodland. Rebecca Nurse started a land dispute of a different nature with your father about two years ago that is still on-going. All of these people are upright people of fine standing in the community, and they all attend church every Sunday. But—all of them are now in the dungeon awaiting trial for witchcraft."

Ruth scowled. "There you go again, talking about my father as though he is involved with nasty things."

William finished grooming the horse. He hung up the tack and then turned to face her. "Ruth," he said gently, "your father wasn't in the courtroom when you were on trial."

"He must have had a good reason," Ruth thrust out her chin in defiance.

"I'm sure he did," William's voice was still gentle.

Then Ruth said, "Those children really were sick. I saw Betty Parris myself when she was stricken. No one can fake those symptoms."

"Oh, Betty and the others were sick all right," he agreed, "at least, in the beginning. It could very well be that afterwards, some people realized that the situation could be manipulated to gain an advantage."

William straightened up, stretched, and then faced her. "You need time to get used to some new ideas. But for now, let's relax."

He took her hand. She stood there, very conscious of his touch upon her fingers. He gripped her hand a bit tighter; not hard enough to hurt, but firmly.

She looked down at his hand clasping hers. Then she looked up into his face, noticing once again how handsome he was. The color of his eyes matched the color of his hair: light brown flecked with gold. She looked deep into his eyes, and felt mesmerized. She couldn't look anywhere else but into his eyes.

He stepped closer to her, and she didn't back away. Instinctively she knew that he was going to touch her, but still she didn't back away.

He gently let go of her hand and tentatively put his arms around her shoulders, as though testing her reaction. When she stood her ground, he tightened his arms and held her close.

She stood there, leaning against him, her head on his chest. She listened to his heartbeat and wondered how fast her own heart was beating. She could smell him, and he smelled like leather. It was a masculine fragrance. Ruth realized that she was glad to be held in William's strong arms.

It didn't feel scandalous at all.

It felt right.

In fact, it felt more than right. She felt a longing in her loins.

He took her chin in one hand and raised her face to meet his own. His lips brushed hers and she trembled in anticipation. Then William pressed his lips upon hers, and she tasted him, felt the firmness of his lips, and felt his tongue taste her own lips.

She experienced a strong yearning as he touched her teeth with his tongue, and then he softly moved his lips upon hers in a slight circular motion. Finally he stopped kissing her, and she kept her face upturned, her eyes closed, hoping he would do it again.

He caressed her neck gently with his fingertips, and Ruth held her breath. She didn't want to move for fear he would stop. She kept her eyes closed, concentrating on the feel of his touch. She was surprised and thrilled when suddenly she felt William lean forward to kiss her neck. He kept kissing her neck, softly brushing his lips down to the hollow in her throat between her collarbones. He stopped kissing and then she felt him run his fingers over the collar of her dress. Would he begin to unbutton it?

Ruth felt stimulated in places she had never before realized could have feelings in her body. She found herself aching for more, not knowing what would come next, but feeling quite sure that something good *should* come next.

Instead he let her go and stepped back. Ruth opened her eyes, and saw that he was standing away from her, looking at her and smiling slightly. Ruth found herself feeling disappointed that the mood was broken.

"You didn't run away from me this time," William said.

"No, I didn't," she smiled back, still feeling a bit shaky from what had just happened.

"I don't think a barn is good enough for you," he said. "But there will be another place for us, and when we are married, we will finish what we started. Here, give me your hand again."

He led her out of the barn, and she was disappointed. She felt a wetness between her legs, and wondered what could have happened after the kiss. She found herself anticipating another intimate encounter.

She was tantalized by the memory of what had just happened in the barn, and was very conscious of his touch as he held her hand. Her thoughts drifted, and she wondered, *What would the touch of his hand feel like upon my body?*

She numbly followed William, wishing he would change his mind and take her back into the barn. But he had spoken of marriage for a second time, and she was beginning to think he actually meant it.

Then she became grateful that he had not taken her in the barn, because despite her newly-found convictions that she would lead a new and braver sort of life, her Puritan upbringing still whispered in her ear that intimacy without marriage was a sin.

She blinked in the sunlight. She knew it would be April very soon. Already the early wildflowers were trying to break dormancy, nestled in the brown, winter-burned grass. She knew that the grass would become green again within weeks.

Ruth walked through the field, holding William's hand, and thought, *It almost doesn't seem real that just yesterday, I was in a dungeon, preparing to die. Today I feel so alive. And I am walking next to a wonderful man, holding his hand. I hope to marry William Porter.*

Then Ruth had another thought, *What about the others that are still in that dungeon?*

"William," she said as she walked alongside him, "There's a four-year-old child in that dungeon underneath the Village jail."

He kept walking, almost leading her through the uneven grass, but looked at her through the corner of his eye. "And?"

"Well," she continued, "think about it. That poor child is suffering in that dungeon. Her name is Dorcas, the daughter of that beggarwoman, Goody Good. Can we help that little girl?"

"Ruth," William said, "it was very dangerous just to get *you* out. Are you saying you want me to go through that risk again for somebody else?"

"And Tituba Indian," Ruth went on as though she hadn't heard what William had said. "I could have done more to help her during her trial. I was too afraid to speak up. Now I realize that I was so very wrong to keep silent. I need to do something to stop the injustices if I can. It wouldn't be just you taking another risk. I'd help."

"I told you that I'm attending meetings with the group of

citizens who are trying to stop the injustices," William said. "I'm doing all I can to help these people."

"But," Ruth persisted, "in the meantime, a four-year-old child is suffering." She stopped walking and looked at him. "Isn't there anything we can do?"

William rolled his eyes. "Why stop at Dorcas Good?" he asked. "Why not spring them all out of jail? The Proctors and Rebecca Nurse and George Jacobs and all the rest? Why, I could sneak them out on fifteen horses and nobody would notice."

She grinned at him, seeing his point. "Okay, I know it's unrealistic to try to rescue everybody. But you bribed a jailer for me, so couldn't we try it just one more time? Just for one more person?"

"The child?"

"Yes, for the child."

"Well," William mused, "we'd have to do some pretty intense planning."

Ruth smiled, her heart soaring. "Does that mean you'll consider it?"

"I'll consider it."

He took her hand and once again began leading her through the field towards the grove of trees, where the Green house lay beyond. She looked around, and realized that the land on which she was walking was of very good quality. She figured that Daniel Green must be very wealthy indeed to own four hundred acres of this fertile land.

When they entered the tree line, they had no problems navigating through the underbrush because it was not yet the time of year for the thickets to become dense. Wildlife was coming out of hibernation, and a rabbit burst out of the bushes, flushed out by their approach.

When they reached the other side of the grove, Ruth got her first glimpse of the Green house. She felt greatly impressed by what she saw.

The house seemed huge. Unlike most Puritan houses, this one was graced with a jutting overhang that framed the doorway.

Two wooden pillars supported the stoop and there was a small stone archway directly in front of the door. It was a pretty house, painted brown with white wooden shutters on the windows.

"What does Daniel Green farm?" Ruth asked William as they approached the front door.

"Mostly wheat, but some rye," William answered as he knocked. "The crops are there in the field to our right. Also, Green has a lot of trees there to our left, so he is involved in the lumber trade, too. But most of the wealth possessed by his family was brought over with him from England."

The door swung open and a young servantmaid answered. She was a girl of about sixteen who had reddish-brown hair tucked into a severe bun, which was the accepted style. A black hat covered her head. "Master William, come in. Mister Green is expecting you."

They entered the formal entranceway where coats were to be hung. William helped Ruth with her cloak and hung it up for her. Then he said, "This is the house where you'll be staying for a while, until things calm down and you can be acquitted. And," William added, "this is the place where you will get quite an education about the politics of Salem Village."

"Why is that?" Ruth asked.

"Because this is the house where the meetings are held. This is the place where plans are being made to put a stop to the Salem witch trials."

"That's right," came a voice. Ruth looked up to see a young man dressed somberly in black, holding the door to the parlor open. He had dark brown hair and matching eyes. His beard was sparse because of his youth, and his face was smooth and unlined.

"This is Joseph Green." William introduced Ruth to the young man who was still holding the parlor door open as a welcoming gesture. "Joseph, this is Ruth Putnam."

Joseph's eyebrows raised. "Putnam?"

William grinned. "Yes, Joseph, this is one Putnam who is joining the Porters."

Chapter Fourteen

They sat at the dining room table, making plans until late into the night.

The next morning, Ruth opened her eyes and was momentarily confused as to her surroundings. But then she relaxed with the knowledge that she was safe. She looked around at the guest room in which she had spent the night. This bedroom was much larger than her accommodations had been at the Parris household. Unlike her last stay, this bedroom had sitting chairs. The curtains were a cheery yellow, and they were parted to let the early spring sunshine enter and warm the room.

Ruth lay in bed, remembering the conversations held in the Green dining room just the night before.

"It was my idea to rescue Dorcas Good," Ruth had said, "so I should be able to come along to help."

"You are a woman," Joseph Green had argued, "and women shouldn't do a man's job."

"I am as old as you are," countered Ruth, "and I am as brave as any man."

"I don't want you to go," William had joined in, "because I don't want anything bad to happen to you. You've already been through enough."

"Thank you for your concern for my welfare," Ruth told William, "but nothing would happen to me because we all would go to Salem Village together. There is strength and safety in numbers."

During the previous night, no matter how much Ruth had pleaded her case, neither Joseph nor William would agree with her. In the end, neither wanted Ruth to accompany their mission to rescue little Dorcas Good.

"You should be glad that we're going to do it," Joseph had said. "Your part in all this was to give us the idea. You were right that a child should not be suffering. There is no way an innocent child should have to endure the conditions of the dungeon just because the Villagers have lost their senses."

Even William, who was very obvious in his affection for her, would not back down.

So as Ruth lay in her new, temporary bedroom on that sunny spring morning, she began to formulate her own plans, separate from those of William and Joseph. She knew she had to help.

Ruth spent the day in repose, reading and sewing. She tried very hard to act normal, like there was nothing on her mind except what was happening in the moment. William took her around the property in a brief tour, but at noon, he saddled his horse and rode to Salem Village. She assumed that William went to somehow place the bribe to the jailer, or perhaps he was going to pay someone else to make the inducement. The exact plans which had been formulated by William and Joseph had not been shared with her. She only knew that the two men were planning to leave the Green farm at midnight to ride to Salem Village without her.

When nightfall finally arrived, Ruth found herself back in the bedroom, watching the moon outside her window. She thought about her situation.

She remembered the pact that she had made to herself that, in the future, she would not be so trusting in other people's opinions unless it made sense to her. She decided that, from now on, she would be braver and more vocal in her own opinions whenever she saw injustices. Perhaps she could make a difference in some of life's outcomes.

So she contemplated two things. The first was that the opinions of William and Joseph that she, being a woman, was too delicate to participate in the rescue were not valid opinions. The second thing that Ruth contemplated was that she would do anything she could to make a difference in outcomes. And that meant participating in the rescue of Dorcas Good.

She was not about to sleep through the night and do nothing.

She decided she would follow the two men when they rode.

The full moon made her nervous. She understood that the bright glow it cast would make it harder to remain concealed when she left the Green house. But when midnight approached, Ruth knew it was time to go. She was determined to carry out her plans and refused to let fear overtake her.

She was warmly dressed and made sure she wore firm, buttoned-down shoes that had low heels and sturdy soles. She cracked open the wooden bedroom door to take a look out into the hallway. She was on the second floor, and she recognized that one of the risks of being caught included getting out of the house itself.

Nobody was in sight, and Ruth desperately hoped that all members of the Green household would be asleep except for William and Joseph. The hallway was cold, lit by a candle in a holder attached to the wall but not warmed by it. The candle released its smoke into the hall, causing the wall above it to be covered with a fine layer of soot.

Pulling her coat tightly around her, Ruth ventured into the hallway. She welcomed the dimness of the hall to help camouflage her escape, but a few feet away from the single candle, the hall was very black. Ruth battled fear because her imagination created all sorts of vile images as to what could be lurking in the dark corners.

She reached the main stairwell. She felt the pounding of her heart and she wondered if she would lose her battle with fear. Paranoia gripped her tightly, and her chest felt constricted so that she couldn't take a deep breath. She was desperately hoping that she would not be observed as she made her way to the first floor of the Green house.

Hastening down the stairs, she was aware that she was not at all familiar with the layout of the house. Ruth thought, *Wouldn't it be ironic if I fell and broke my neck, dying before I even had a chance to get to the Salem Village jail where the real danger is supposed to be?* But she made it to the bottom safely, and continued quickly across the first floor until she reached the front door. She opened it softly, praying it would not creak. Then she found herself on the stone archway between the two wooden pillars.

Ruth hurried across the front yard, through the grass that was wet with dew. The dew sparkled from the moon's glow, and the beauty of the crisp spring night struck her. The air was damp but smelled sweet, and she heard an early-season screech owl shrill as it hunted rodents in the darkness.

She also heard male voices up ahead. She strained her eyes to see in the moonlight and then she spotted the two men entering the grove of trees. She knew that they were headed towards the barn to saddle their horses for their midnight ride.

Ruth suddenly realized that she hadn't counted the number of horses in that barn. She had understandably been distracted by William's kisses when she had been there before. What if there was no horse left over for her?

But it was too late to worry about that. Determined not to let anything stop her, she continued forward. She was glad she was wearing such dark clothes, and hoped she could blend into the night. She reached the grove of trees and tried once again to listen for William and Joseph, but this time she heard nothing.

There! Ruth heard a twig snap ahead. This gave her perspective as to how fast she should go to maintain a safe distance behind the two men. She didn't want to be close enough to get caught following, but she didn't want to be far enough behind to lose them, either.

Once she entered the grove of trees, she realized just how sinister darkness could seem. With tree branches creating a canopy that blocked the moonlight, the wooded area was strange and foreboding. The crickets had not yet emerged from hibernation, so it was unnaturally still.

Ruth treaded carefully, making her way through the underbrush slowly. She knew that if she fell and twisted her ankle, she would wind up spending the night there because no one would look for her until late the next morning.

But she continued forward, making every attempt to continue in a straight path towards the direction where she had last heard William and Joseph. Finally she emerged on the other side of the shallow grove of trees, and instantly the moonlight appeared incredibly bright in contrast to the dark wooded area.

She spied the two men close to the barn, and the moonlight created long shadows upon the meadow in their wake, as though they were being followed by dark stripes. In the moonlight, there was no sense of color, and everything appeared as though shades of gray. Ruth stood in one spot until she saw the men enter the barn, and then she began to run.

She heard the stiff winter-burned meadow grass crunch beneath her feet as she sprinted. She was glad she had chosen her shoes carefully, for she was sure-footed and fleet.

Reaching the barn, Ruth chose a side away from the entrance. She hid, pressing herself against the wall. She was panting slightly but forced herself to breathe through her nose and not her mouth so she wouldn't make any sounds.

She heard William and Joseph talking, but couldn't make out the words. She strained to listen, hoping that she could hear them verbalizing their plans. But it was not to be.

Soon the young men rode from the barn, and both of their horses began to canter across the meadow. As William and Joseph rode away, Ruth knew it was time to enter the barn herself.

She would have to be very, very quick.

She didn't want to be left behind.

So she raced into the barn. She ran to the stall where William had unsaddled his horse just the day before yesterday, but of course that stall was empty. She whirled around, frantically trying to see in the dark barn, looking for another horse.

Then she heard a snorting sound coming from a corner, followed by a soft whinny. Ruth ran towards the sound, and discovered that in a corner stall was another horse.

But when she saw the animal her heart sank, because this

horse was so light-colored that it was almost white. This horse could be seen very well in the moonlight. And it seemed unusually large.

Still, it was the only horse left. Horses were expensive, and most farmers had only a few. When Ruth examined this horse closer, her dismay grew. This horse was a draft animal, one normally used to pull a plow.

But she told herself that a horse was a horse.

She grabbed the bridle and almost threw it on the animal. She quickly scanned the stall for a saddle, and was surprised that there was indeed a saddle big enough for a draft horse. The horse seemed gentle, and Ruth thought that maybe God smiled upon her after all.

Once the horse was ready, she led the big animal to the door of the barn, then mounted. She had ridden often on her father's farm, but until her wild ride with William, she had never ridden with each leg straddled over either side. Women always rode side-saddle. Now Ruth chose to ride as would a man, because she realized that it would assist with keeping her balance. She might need that little extra help tonight.

She flung the reins and the horse began to gallop. It lumbered clumsily as its oversized hooves pounded the earth. Even though she bounced up and down in the saddle in response to the draft horse's rough gait, she knew that at that pace, she would quickly close the distance between she and the two men.

And soon she spotted them up ahead. So she stopped her horse and let them once again travel out of sight so that she wouldn't be detected. Then she flicked the reins and followed at a slow trot.

An hour went by, and Ruth still followed. She passed the first of the farms that lay on the outskirts of Salem Village and recognized that she was getting close. But once she entered the Village boundary, she picked up her pace. She wanted to reach the jail at the same time the men did.

Most of the streets in the Village were dirt, but the main street was cobbled. Ruth dismounted about two blocks away from the jail and tied her large, white draft horse to a hitching post. She decided it would be much safer to walk the rest of the way, without the hooves of the horse clattering on the cobblestones.

The stars shone like twinkling jewels in the night, and the moonlight made everything appear magical. Ruth's senses were heightened because her jangled nerves pushed the adrenaline through her system. She constantly looked around herself as she advanced towards the jail.

She slowly approached the building, remaining cautious. But no one was out in front.

Oh no, she thought, *did I lose William and Joseph? Did they already accomplish what they came for? Am I too late?*

But then a new idea hit her. *Of course,* she thought. *They wouldn't go around to the front of the jail; they would attempt a rescue from behind.*

So she began to move again, carefully picking her way and remaining close to the building so that she could be enveloped within the shadows of the night. When she made her way to the rear of the jail, she saw two shapes in the moonlight and knew she was not too late after all; for there were William and Joseph.

She stood still for a few minutes, observing. It appeared that the two men were standing underneath a rear window of the jail, with their heads close together, whispering between themselves. The window was placed high off the ground, at a level of about seven feet up. And—the window was very small.

Finally Ruth could stand it no longer. She decided to expose her presence. After all, what could the men do to her now, at this point? Tell her to go home? If so, she would refuse.

So she stepped out of the shadows, and the two men were so startled by the presence of another that they jumped visibly. "Who goes there?" she heard William's voice.

"It's Ruth," she identified herself.

"Ruth!" Joseph softly exclaimed. "What are you doing here? We told you to stay out of it. This is no place for a woman."

"Let her stay," William commanded, and Ruth was completely surprised. "Maybe she can get through this window.

Only a small person could fit."

"What!" Joseph was incredulous.

"What do you want me to do?" Ruth stepped closer to the two men until she also stood under the window.

"We bribed the jailer to open the back door for us tonight," William explained, "yet when we got here, we found that not only is the back door still locked, but the jailer is nowhere to be found. He's simply not here. I'm thinking that there is probably no one at all inside the jail except for the prisoners. Now, that's both good and bad. Good because whichever one of us that can get inside can move more openly, but bad because maybe none of us can get inside at all."

"Do you think this window is unlocked?" Ruth asked.

"Maybe," William answered, "or maybe not. If not, you can break the glass. That is, if you're willing to do this."

Joseph was still disbelieving. "You're really going to let a woman do a man's job?"

"We need her," William said simply, "and besides, Ruth knows the layout of the jail and the dungeon. After all, she's been inside before, so she could be in and out more quickly than you or I could."

Joseph looked at Ruth doubtfully. "All right," he finally consented, "but only because we don't have much time. Someone is surely going to come soon."

William looked at Ruth. "Are you willing to do this?"

"Lift me to the window." That was her answer.

"We'll lift you," William told her. Then he slowly said, "But first, I want to give you a gun."

"A gun!" Ruth spoke softly, yet her voice revealed the anxiety she felt. "I don't know how to use a gun. Even if I did know how, I don't think I could."

"You probably won't need it," William soothed her, "but I think you should have it with you anyway. It's a dangerous thing you're about to do, and I told you before that I care about you. Please, take the gun."

She didn't say anything, but nodded.

"This is a flintlock," William said, as he showed her the pistol. Its seven-inch barrel looked fat to her. William showed her the main parts of the pistol, and explained to her how to draw the hammer to its full-cocked position. He showed her how to hold her hands for the steadiest aim, and also how to pull the trigger. Then he said, "It's already loaded and ready to fire, but remember—you only have one shot, so if you have to use it, be sure to aim carefully first."

Ruth grimaced. She thought to herself, *I can't do that. I can't fire a gun.* But because it seemed so important to William, she took it. She put it deep within a pocket of her cloak, being careful not to dislodge the powder in its priming pan.

In the moonlight, William and Joseph locked fingers. Ruth stepped primly on top of their gripped hands and felt herself being lifted. Almost dizzy with adrenaline, she soon found herself shoulder-high with the window.

She leaned forward and tried to lift the sash. It was initially stuck, but then surprisingly it lifted easily. She was buoyed by the fact that the window was not locked. Once she pushed it open, she tried to hoist herself onto the window sill. William and Joseph lifted her higher, and she managed to pull herself until she was half inside, her pelvis still on the ledge.

Ruth twisted her body around until she could bring her legs up. The men had been right; only a small person could squeeze into this diminutive opening. But she raised her knees up and compressed herself until she managed to push her way through the window.

The next thing she knew was that she was sitting with her legs on the inside of the room, hunched over in the small space, and facing the room.

But then there was the problem that the window was so high off the ground. *What should I do?* she wondered. *Should I jump? What if I hurt myself?*

Visions of herself lying helplessly on the wooden floor of the jail with a broken leg passed through her mind.

Instead of jumping, Ruth again twisted her torso. She

managed to turn herself around so that she could hold onto the window sill and let her body hang over the edge. Then she dropped safely the rest of the way.

The thudding sound of her feet contacting with the floor seemed loud to her, and it sent her heart racing. She stood there a moment, leaning against the wall, trying to collect herself. Then she turned around to see what she could see.

There were two candles lit inside the room, so it was light enough to see perfectly well. The first place Ruth looked was at the trap door to the dungeon. She quietly gasped as she realized that the trap door was open.

That meant there was a jailer in the dungeon. A lawman was here after all!

But she took strength from the idea that this must be the same jailer that William had bribed. She hoped that this jailer would not stop her efforts.

She looked at the back door, and saw that it was chained shut. The lock required a key. Her gaze drifted to the trap door again, and she wondered, *If this is the same jailer that was bribed, why didn't he unlock the back door which was the original agreement?*

Could this be a different jailer?

Ruth heard sounds drifting up from the dungeon, and one of the noises sounded like a crying child. Her mind became set. She would take the chance. She would venture into the dungeon. But her hand was in her pocket, clutching the gun. Suddenly she realized that she was very glad she had that gun.

Ruth walked over to the trap door and peered inside, down the wooden steps. She could see a flickering light, and realized that there was a candle lit down there. How different it was when she spent a night of pitch blackness in that terrible dungeon!

Her mind raced. Could she try to free everybody who was doomed and chained in that horrible hole?

But reason prevailed, and she knew that on this particular trip, she could only save one person, if indeed she could save anyone at all.

It would be the child. Ruth believed that every one of the prisoners was innocent; but a child was the most innocent of all.

She tentatively stepped into the dark abyss, and carefully navigated the steep wooden steps. The stench of the dungeon almost overwhelmed her, and she felt like swooning. She could hear the dripping water, and she could hear the prisoners who were softly moaning, expressing their utter misery. She could hear chains rattle. But suddenly there was a different sound.

"Stay away from me!" Ruth heard a woman's cry, and she realized it was Bridget Bishop's voice.

"Leave her alone!" Ruth then heard a man shout, and recognized that voice as belonging to John Proctor.

"And just how do you intend to stop me, old man? You going to cast a spell on me?" The man who was speaking began to laugh.

Ruth's eyes began to adjust to the dark cellar. The candle illuminated the dungeon just enough for her to realize what was going on. The jailer had Bridget pushed against a wet wall, and he was groping her. He had pulled one side of her dress over the shoulder, and it exposed bare skin. He was pushing himself on the young woman who was vainly trying to fend him off, but Bridget's hands were restricted because of the shackles binding her wrists.

Now Ruth was very glad she had the gun. Slowly she pulled it out of her pocket and took aim just the way William had shown her.

"Get away from Bridget," Ruth commanded in a strong, steady voice.

"Go to hell where you belong," the man said as he continued his maneuverings upon Bridget Bishop, not seeing who was talking to him.

"I will shoot."

The jailer whirled around to see which prisoner had to gall to confront him and say she had a gun. Visibility was good in the flickering candlelight. When he saw Ruth, what began as a sneer on the jailer's face quickly changed into an expression of wide-eyed surprise.

Then he scowled. "You can't shoot me—you're just a woman."

"I know how to use this gun and I will if I have to."

The jailer chose to believe her. "Don't shoot."

"Get away from her," Ruth ordered.

She scanned the dungeon, trying to spot Dorcas Good while still keeping the gun aimed at the jailer. So far Ruth had not found it necessary to cock it, because the jailer remained frozen in place.

She said to Bridget, "Can you help me?"

Bridget straightened her dress. "What do you need?"

"Bring me the child."

But when Bridget picked Dorcas Good off of the wet, cold dungeon floor, the child began screaming. "I want my mama! I want my mama!"

Sarah Good was still chained to the wall. "Dorcas, honey, go with the lady," the beggarwoman crooned to comfort her little girl. "Mama will follow you soon. Go now. I tell you to go with the lady."

"Mama, you will leave here soon?"

"Yes, Dorcas, now go with the lady."

Little Dorcas reluctantly made her way to where Ruth was standing. The chains on her wrists seemed oversized to confine such tiny hands, and they weighed heavy upon the child's arms. Tears streamed down the small face, and the little girl continued to whimper.

Ruth grabbed the upper flesh of the child's arm because she didn't want to take any chances that Dorcas would run back to her mother. She held the gun with the other hand. "You come too," Ruth said to Bridget.

"What about my wife?" wailed John Proctor. "Take her with you too!"

"And me!" cried Elizabeth Howe.

"And me!" cried George Jacobs.

"Please take me!" came a surge of pleading voices. "Please!

Please! Take me too! Please, oh please!"

"I can't!" Ruth cried, and the tears streamed freely down her own cheeks. "I can't take you all! I swear I can't! I swear I can't!"

"Then we'll die!" the voices cried; so many voices. "You can't leave us all here to die! We're innocent! We'll be murdered!"

Ruth began loudly sobbing. She grabbed little Dorcas and ran up the wooden stairs in a desperate retreat. Bridget was right on her heels. Ruth pulled Dorcas into her arms and carried the child the rest of the way as she raced up the creaky, unstable wooden steps. She heard chains rattle behind her as prisoners began to follow.

Ruth burst through the trap door, and Bridget followed, leaping to the upper floor. Ruth heard others climbing after them, and weeping, she closed the trap door, imprisoning the accused witches once again in the dungeon below.

Ruth knew it would condemn them all to try to rescue more than one person. It would condemn William and Joseph. Already she was taking Bridget with her, and Ruth knew that the risk of rescuing a second person would probably be her own downfall.

Suddenly she could hear the front door to the jail being unlocked. She heard male voices and her heart sank. They were coming. She was about to be caught. She was doomed, and so were Dorcas and Bridget.

But she decided to keep going until someone actually put his hands on her to physically stop her. "Quick!" she cried. "Help me push Dorcas up through this window!"

Ruth had no time to consider anything. She only knew that she had to keep going.

"She'll fall on the other side!" Bridget exclaimed. "Dorcas is so little—a fall like that could kill her."

"No," Ruth said, "there's someone on the other side to catch her."

So they pushed the little girl up though the window, ignoring the child's cries of terror. Ruth pushed blindly; desperately hoping that it was true that William and Joseph were still outside the window to catch the child. If not, would dying in a fall be preferable to death by hanging?

There was no time to think, only to act. Ruth was so very, very desperate.

"You go next," Bridget offered, and Ruth grabbed a chair. She began to climb up onto the window sill, and Bridget helped to push.

But at that same moment, a group of lawmen burst into the room. Behind her, Ruth felt hands grab for her shoes, but she kicked them away. Closing her eyes, she jumped out of the window, sailing into the night in a lightning-quick descent to the ground.

Chapter Fifteen

She felt arms catch her, but she slammed into William and her breath was knocked from her. She felt him reel slightly backwards with the impact of her body, but he quickly recovered and Ruth knew she was safe in William's arms.

"Where's Dorcas?" she asked as she gulped for air. At the same time she spoke, she could hear the child softly sobbing, a gentle, hiccup-like sound. Ruth was relieved, because a crying child was a child who was still alive.

"They're coming!" Joseph cried. "We've got to run!"

Ruth felt William pull her, and she followed in a dead run. She acted purely on adrenaline without thought.

William leaped upon his horse, then grabbed her arm and swung her on behind him. Joseph did the same with Dorcas, except he put the little girl in front of him, probably fearing she'd fall off otherwise. Both men jerked the reins, and both horses bolted into action, taking off at a full gallop.

Angry voices followed them, but Ruth decided by the time the lawmen went to their own horses to give chase, she and William would have had too great a head start to be caught.

But still they galloped away at the fastest clip possible. After all, the men could always fire muskets.

Ruth desperately hung on to William, burying her face in his back. She knew she would be killed for certain if she fell. She gripped him tightly, interlocking her fingers as though her hands were welded together.

The horse was fleet and the ride was so much smoother than when she had ridden the big white horse.

And then Ruth remembered: the white draft horse! It was still tethered two blocks from the jail. But there was nothing she could do about it now.

After about a mile or so, Ruth felt the pace slow and she knew William must be pulling back on the reins. She lifted her head from where she had buried it into William's back, and looked around.

Joseph was reining in his horse beside them, and she could see that little Dorcas was still sitting in front. Ruth felt gratified that at least her efforts had spared one life from the gallows. She wondered what was happening to Bridget right now, who must have been caught by the lawmen who came in through the front door of the jail when she was making her own escape out the window.

Poor Bridget. Ruth knew that the consequences of trying to escape would be very bad, very bad indeed. She wondered if there would be torture.

"You did a good job," Joseph called to her from his horse.

"Where are we taking Dorcas?" she asked, wishing she had been able to somehow save Bridget too.

"To the Tarbell farm," Joseph answered. "The Tarbells have agreed to hide Dorcas and to care for her as long as necessary."

"Why can't we keep her?" Ruth wanted to know.

"Because we are hiding *you*," Joseph told her, and Ruth could see him grinning in the moonlight.

William half-turned in the saddle. "How did you get to Salem Village? What horse did you ride?"

"The big white draft horse from Joseph's barn. Oh William, that horse is still tied up in the square."

William hesitated, then said, "No one will know who owns the horse."

But Ruth wasn't so sure.

They began moving again, but at a much slower pace. They passed the town of Ipswich, and continued past the Green farm. After over an hour of riding, finally they reached another farm and rode to the house. William brought his horse to a stop and then dismounted. He tied the horse to a post near the front door and then helped Ruth to the ground.

All four went to the front door and knocked.

A middle-aged man answered the door, his face lined from the weather and his dark hair peppered with gray. He was fully dressed, so Ruth knew that despite the odd hour, this man had been up and waiting; expecting them.

"Come in," the man smiled warmly, and instinctively Ruth knew that Dorcas would be in good hands within this household.

William used his key to remove the child's manacles. Ruth saw that the girl's wrists were an angry red color.

A middle-aged woman was standing inside, and she rushed to take Dorcas into her arms. "I'll give her some warm milk and put her to bed," the woman said, then left the entranceway, carrying the little girl.

Mr. Tarbell led them to the dining room. They sat at the table, which was long and crudely carved, and the eight wooden chairs surrounding it were very heavy.

"So this is Ruth Putnam," he said when they were all sitting. He grinned, and the lines around his eyes became even more pronounced.

"How do you do?" Ruth asked primly.

Suddenly Mr. Tarbell's smile vanished and his face became stern. "Do you know what your father is doing?"

Ruth sat up straight in surprise.

"That's not necessary," William hastily interrupted.

"No," Ruth said firmly. She looked at William. "You've been keeping things from me about my father all along. I think you want to protect my feelings. But I'm not a child any longer. I've grown very strong over the past few weeks. I can handle the truth."

William gazed deeply into her eyes for a few minutes, not speaking, but searching for answers nonetheless. Then he seemed to make up his mind, for he turned and nodded at Mr. Tarbell.

"There is a group of citizens who are trying to change the events now happening in Salem Village," Tarbell told her. "William's father, Israel Porter, has taken the lead. We meet at

Joseph's farm."

"I'm aware of those things," Ruth said softly.

The man continued. "One of the accused is Rebecca Nurse. Mrs. Nurse has fertile land that lies between your father's farm and the Frost Fish River. For the last two years, your father has been trying to obtain the Nurse property through lawsuits."

Ruth expected something bad, but not this bad.

Mr. Tarbell hesitated, then said, "John Putnam has been trying to force the Nurses off of the property, but they have so far been able to retain the upper hand. Now, if Rebecca Nurse is convicted of witchcraft, all of her assets will have to be sold to pay for legal costs. Her husband Francis will be forced to move. And your farther has maneuvered to be first in line to purchase the property. You see, that property is valuable, but under the circumstances, will sell very cheaply."

"I see," Ruth said grimly.

"Your father has been dividing up the land he already has between your brothers. Without the Nurse land to add, the existing Putnam land is getting squeezed into such small parcels that each Putnam son has wound up with practically nothing."

Ruth felt sick to her stomach, but said nothing.

"There's more," Tarbell said. "Your father is not as rich as he seems to be."

Ruth paled, remembering that, at one time, Abigail Williams had told her very much the same thing.

Oh! It seemed so long ago now, when Ruth was living at the Parris house, and Abigail had thrust her chin out, her dark eyes flashing, and had said, "Well, let me tell you something else, Miss So-High-and-Mighty. Your father told my uncle that unless you marry, he feels no obligation to give you any parcels of his land. Your father said that his land can only stretch so far, and he has fine sons who need to inherit. Maybe your family isn't as rich as you think they are!"

In her heart, Ruth knew that Mr. Tarbell was telling her the truth.

She waited for more revelations, still not commenting.

"Years ago, John Putnam took a case to the Appellate Court in Boston. Samuel Parris was the jury foreman," Tarbell said. "The outcome of that case, had it gone sour, might have completely bankrupted your father and put him in debtor's prison. But Parris conveniently lost some damaging papers, and so your father won the case. Still, your father never did completely recover financially. He hasn't been as well off as he was before that court case."

"So," Ruth finally spoke, "that's why my father owes Reverend Parris favors. That's why my father petitioned Salem Village to hire Reverend Parris."

"That's enough," William spoke sharply to Tarbell. Then he turned to Ruth. "Are you all right?"

"Yes," Ruth met William's eyes directly. "But all of this means that we have to rescue Rebecca Nurse. I cannot let her blood spill because of my family's corruption."

William said quickly, "Ruth, we can only act within reason."

"When is Rebecca's trial?" Ruth asked.

"In about two weeks," William answered. "But Ruth—"

"I want to attend."

"You can't!" Joseph exclaimed, joining in. "You'd be recognized, then re-arrested!"

"Ruth, think about it," William reasoned. "He's right."

"I *need* to attend," Ruth was adamant. "I need to try to right some wrongs. I can be disguised so that no one would know who I am. I could sit in the back. There's got to be a way I can go to the trial."

Joseph looked at William and grinned. "What kind of woman do you have here?"

William smiled back. "The best kind."

"Oh the young, they feel so invincible," Tarbell said. "At this late hour, we could all use some hot tea and bread."

He rose, and Ruth wondered why there were no servants in the Tarbell household. It would certainly be unusual in a farm of this size.

In a minute, Tarbell returned with mugs and a slab of butter, which he placed on the table. Then he left again to retrieve a pot of tea and a loaf of bread. He also placed these on the table.

"Nothing to eat for me, but I'll take some tea," said William. Joseph said the same thing.

But Ruth was hungry. She took a piece of bread, and noticed it was rye.

Perhaps it was because of all the energy she had expended in the rescue of Dorcas Good, but she realized she was ravenous. Even though she normally turned her nose up at rye bread, Ruth began slathering butter upon a slice.

She bit into it, hoping no one would notice her grimace at the taste. It tasted even bitterer than she remembered rye bread to be. But Ruth ate the entire piece, and even reached for a second.

Finally all rose to leave the Tarbell household. Ruth knew it would be dawn very soon, and she was so tired that she hated the thought of getting back up on the horse. But she pushed herself to stay awake and once more got behind William to ride to the Green farm.

When they arrived, the sun was casting orange and pink hues upon the eastern horizon. The day was beginning, and there was enough light to grant visibility. The trio put the horses in the barn and walked to the grove of trees that led to the Green house.

But when they emerged from the trees, Ruth saw that a man was standing out in front of the Green house. The man held the reins to a horse.

Ruth's blood froze in her veins, because she recognized the horse.

It was the big, white draft horse.

"Get back into the trees," William told her, "and hide until we can find out what this is about."

She did as she was told, and despite her weariness, Ruth crouched behind a bush and waited. William and Joseph left to confront the man holding the draft horse.

The wait seemed endless. But finally the stranger rode off on a horse of his own, and Ruth breathed a sigh of relief. Shortly, William came back to retrieve her.

"Who was that man and what did he want?" Ruth asked, rising from behind the bush.

"You left the horse in the Village?" Joseph answered her question with another question.

"I told you she did," William said.

"Well, you did what you had to do, and I don't blame you," Joseph said. "Still, they know it's my horse. And word about it is going to get back to John Hathorne. There's going to be suspicion that someone from this household was responsible for the jail break earlier tonight."

"I'm so sorry," Ruth said. "What will we do?"

"Nothing," William answered. "We told him someone had stolen that horse. We'll see if Hathorne believes it. Come on, you must be cold. Let's go to the house, and you can get some sleep."

Ruth wanted to do just that. But she wasn't cold; in fact, she felt rather hot. She wondered if she was starting to come down with an illness.

Chapter Sixteen

She lay in bed in the large upstairs room of the Green household.

She could feel the sweat trickle between her breasts and her hair felt wet and plastered to her scalp. She had already thrown off her covers and unbuttoned the top of her nightdress, but there seemed to be no relief from the intense heat that penetrated her very being.

The room was cheerfully bright because the midday sun was streaming through the parted curtains in the window. When Ruth had ridden to the Green house at dawn, she had immediately gone upstairs to her bedroom to try to sleep. But now, sleep evaded her because she felt incredibly sick.

This was not a type of sickness that she had ever before experienced. Her mind was in a dreamlike state that made her feel as though everything was artificial; as though she was viewing herself through someone else's eyes. Yet at the same time, she experienced an underlying feeling of paranoia, a vague expectancy of great doom. She kept thinking that she saw someone in the room out of the corner of her vision, but every time she turned, the room was empty.

Ruth was restless and her fingers and her toes tingled oddly. She had pains in her stomach, and she realized that she was probably very sick.

Then the spasms began.

It started with cramping in her hands and feet. Her fingers and toes seemed to become locked into odd angles. The contortions were painful. After a few minutes, her fingers and toes would relax, but then they would intermittently begin to spasm again.

The uncontrollable movements began to spread. Soon her

arms were acting as though they had a mind of their own, and began to stiffen and lock into place at odd angles. Her legs followed suit, and she found she could no longer bend her knees. But worst of all was that she couldn't seem to close her mouth. Soon she couldn't even swallow. After awhile, she lay helpless as drool dribbled down her chin.

She lay on her back, unable to turn over.

She was very, very frightened.

Had it been true all along? Were there witches in Salem Village? Was she being victimized?

For if this was witchcraft, then it wasn't an illness at all. If this was witchcraft, then she was a victim of assault, and that was a crime.

Could it be possible that the accused witches in the Salem Village dungeon really belonged there? Were they witches after all, and not the innocents that she had previously believed? Were they angry that she had not been able to rescue them all, and were now getting their revenge?

No. Ruth couldn't believe any of that.

She chose not to believe in Salem witches because she understood through all that she had learned that there were other reasons for the accusations of witchcraft, and that these other reasons had nothing to do with witches.

The reasons why the Village people were suffering in the dungeon were for reasons such as political corruption, landowner greed, and desire for attention by the accusers. Ruth had seen most of these things first hand, and had believed William's explanations for the rest.

There was a knock on the door. She tried to open her mouth to speak, but she heard weird noises coming out of her own mouth. She moaned "Uhh, uhh, uhh" and remembered that the same foreign sounds had been uttered by Betty Parris when the ten-year-old child had been so very ill.

And so Ruth knew that she had the same sickness as had Betty.

The important thing was: Betty Parris had survived the

illness.

The knock sounded on the door again, a bit more urgently. Then a soft voice asked, "Mistress Ruth? Are you awake?"

Ruth recognized the voice as the young red-haired servantmaid who attended to the Green household. But try as she might, Ruth was unable to maneuver her tongue to form words.

When no more knocks followed, Ruth's heart sank. She was afraid that the servantmaid assumed she was fast asleep and therefore was not to be disturbed. In reality, Ruth was very frightened, and wanted someone to know of her desperate situation. She wished she could run to the door, open it, and call for help.

Instead, another convulsion racked her arms and legs. She felt herself twisting into painful positions, as the sweat trickled down her brow. She suffered the stinging salt in her eyes because she was unable to perform the simple act of wiping her face with her hand.

Suddenly there was another knock on her door, and she heard William's voice. "Is everything all right in there?"

"Uhhh, uhhh, uhhhh..." Ruth tried to call out, but it sounded more like a steer in the field than a human voice.

"I'm sending the servant inside your bedroom," William sounded tense.

The door opened, and the young servantmaid began to rush in, but then stopped in her tracks in shock. "Master William, you must come here!" the red-haired girl exclaimed.

Ruth managed to turn her head to see William enter the bedroom. She saw his eyes grow wide in his face, his expression one of extreme surprise.

But her vision was distorted and when she looked at him. William's face seemed to expand and contract. Colorful, dancing lights appeared to flicker around his head, and she wondered if William was surrounded by the halo of Heaven.

As he approached her bed, Ruth saw that there seemed to be duplicates of William following his every movement. Nothing in the room appeared as though solid; objects rippled and seemed translucent. Everything appeared more colorful than reality; bright and glowing.

She wondered if she had been wrong in her assessment that since Betty Parris had survived the illness, then so would she. She wondered if in fact she had already died, and this was either Heaven or Hell.

Ruth felt disembodied, and her bedroom seemed far away. It was as though she was a ship adrift, with no anchor to the shore that was reality. Her feet and hands burned and she could not seem to control the involuntary movements of her limbs. She imagined demons in her room, but at the same time, she was sure she saw angels hovering around her bed.

She looked at William, and through her confusion, could not decide if he was a devil or an angel.

And as William stood above her bed, appearing to shimmer with flickering lights around him, Ruth lost consciousness.

Gradually Ruth began to come back to reality as her illness subsided. Her fingers and toes began to tingle instead of burn, and she regained control of her muscles. She felt a bit better each day. Eventually she was able to sit up in bed and sip the soup that the servantmaid provided.

William and Joseph sat in chairs next to her bed.

"What do you think was wrong with me?" Ruth asked.

"I think you had Saint Anthony's Fire," William responded.

"What's that? Saint Anthony's Fire? I've never heard of it," Ruth was puzzled.

"Well," William told her, "no one knows what causes it. But there's been writing about it. The first time the Fire was mentioned in history was about five hundred years ago in a town in France called Pont Saint Esprit. A lot of the townsfolk were afflicted with the same symptoms that you had. It's happened off and on ever since; in Europe, anyway. I've never heard of it happening here in the New World before. At least, until now."

"So you think that Betty Parris and Ann Putnam had Saint Anthony's Fire?" Ruth asked. "And the others, too?"

"Well, I sure don't believe that they were bewitched by Tituba Indian," William said.

He added, "While you were sick, we rubbed pig fat on your hands and feet. That's the only known treatment for Saint Anthony's Fire, because pig fat reduces the swelling."

"Another treatment is God's mercy," Joseph added. He had a Bible in his lap.

William smiled. "Joseph has been praying for you every hour during your illness."

"In the day when I cried thou answered me, and strengthened my soul," Joseph Green read from the Bible, "He healeth the broken in heart, and bindeth up their wounds. And He touched her hand, and the fever left her, and she arose, and ministered unto them."

Joseph continued, "For we are saved by hope. For God hath not given us the spirit of fear, but of power, and of love, and of a sound mind."

Ruth felt moved by the reading. How much more beautiful the Word of God could be when read by someone who sought the inspirational and fundamental aspects of the Good Book. Reverend Parris had only sought out the darkest passages in the Bible to validate his hate.

She remembered Saint Matthew, where it was written: *But whosoever will be great among you, let him be your minister*. She remembered that William had once told her: "There is another man who should be appointed minister of Salem Village. A *real* man of God, not an impostor like Parris."

William had said those words when she had secretly met him in the Parris barn, the first time he had ever kissed her. She understood now that William had meant Joseph Green.

How long ago that day in the Parris barn seemed! She remembered that when William had kissed her the very first time, she had run away. Ruth decided that she would never run from William ever again.

She smiled at William as he sat in a chair next to Joseph. He had been concentrating; listening to Joseph's reading, but he caught her glance.

William smiled back at her, and Ruth wondered if she saw love in his eyes. She hoped she would soon become his wife, and then she would find out what comes next, after a kiss.

Chapter Seventeen

She dressed carefully, covering the lower portion of her face with a scarf-like shawl. Ruth figured that since it was only the end of April, it was still chilly enough that wearing a shawl would not attract undue attention. She carefully placed a starched, white hat on her head, pushed forward to shade her eyes.

Joseph Green's mother was named Mary. The older woman was a size or two larger than herself, so Ruth borrowed a dress from Mary and lined it with linen. The extra cloth made Ruth appear as though she weighed more than she did.

When her costume was complete, Ruth scrutinized herself in a looking glass. She peered at herself from every angle until she was convinced that any Villager would be hard-pressed to recognize her true identity. Plus, Ruth was hoping that not only would she be unnoticed as she sat in the very rear of the courtroom, but also that the crowd would be so interested in the trial, they would not pay attention to anything else.

Ruth was getting ready to attend the trial of Rebecca Nurse.

She knew that all of the accused witches in the dungeon were having their worldly possessions sold in their absence. It was Puritan law that whoever was jailed was required to pay for their own upkeep.

She was hoping that it was not too late; that Rebecca Nurse had not already had all of her possessions sold right out from under her. She was hoping that the trial would be completed before the prisoner's costs could escalate to such an amount that the entire farm would have to be sold to compensate.

Ruth knew that if Rebecca's land were sold, her own father would be standing first in line to purchase it for a cutthroat price.

ACCUSED: A TALE OF THE SALEM WITCH TRIALS

And Ruth was determined not to let that happen.

Finally she felt she was ready to leave the bedroom. She walked down the hall and descended the stairs. When she reached the bottom of the staircase, William and Joseph were waiting for her.

"How do I look?" Ruth asked them.

Joseph grinned. "Who are *you?*"

Ruth saw William's jaw drop open in surprise, and that made her quite sure that her identity would remain hidden.

"You can close your mouth now," she teased him.

"It's just that you look so different," William told her.

"Good," she smiled, "because that's the point."

"Okay, Miss Whoever-You-Are," William smiled back, "I suppose I'll admit that your plan just might work after all."

Joseph chose to remain at his father's farm, not wanting to attend the trial. Although William rode with Ruth, when they reached the border of Salem Village, they would separate. The plan was that Ruth was to sit in the very back of the courtroom, and William was to sit with his father, Israel Porter. Once they reached Salem Village, Ruth and William would pretend not to know each other. They both knew it was necessary for Ruth's safety, but William was not happy about it.

"If something happens to you, how would I know?" he complained when they reached the Salem Village boundary.

"You'd know because I wouldn't be in the courtroom."

"I don't like this."

"It will be all right," she assured him, just before he rode off without her. Alone, she sat still and waited calmly upon her standing horse, basking in the spring sunlight and listening to birds sing. She waited patiently until about twenty minutes had passed. Then she clucked to the horse and shook the reins.

The horse she rode was a brown mare, recently purchased by the Greens from a neighboring farm. She smiled when she thought of the difference between the new horse and that big white draft animal she had ridden the last time she was in Salem

Village.

Finally she reached the courthouse. Ruth discovered that there were no spaces left to tether her brown mare. All of the hitching posts seemed to be already filled with horses tied to the rail—so many horses! She thought to herself, *The entire Village must be here.*

She rode a few blocks until she finally found an unused post. She dismounted and securely tied her horse. Then she began to walk back to the courthouse, primly lifting her skirt so as not to drag her dress though the mud of the street.

When she entered the courthouse, she looked around with nervousness. The unyielding wooden pews were jammed with spectators, and in front of the seating area was the dark wooden railing to hold people back. As was every time she had been to the witch trials, there was no jury. There was a wooden platform in front, and upon it was the box for the magistrate to sit and reign over the courtroom. Directly alongside the magistrate's chair was the witness chair.

This time it was Rebecca Nurse who looked frightened and bewildered as she sat in the witness chair for the entire Village to see and scorn.

Ruth found a space on a pew placed against the rear wall of the courthouse. She quickly sat and was relieved when no one bothered to notice her. None of the attending Villagers even paid her a passing glance.

So far so good.

Ruth looked at Rebecca Nurse, the sad figure sitting in the witness chair.

Rebecca wore a brown dress that had once tightly fitted a plump frame, but now the clothing hung loose and lifeless upon a body that had lost twenty pounds. The woman was middle-aged and had looked her years a month ago, but now appeared almost old, drawn and haggard. The month Rebecca had spent in prison had given her complexion a gray appearance, and there were dark smudges underneath her eyes.

Ruth pulled her scarf closer around her chin, and observed the room in front of her. The courtroom was jammed with spectators, and it was becoming standing room only. She realized that she had made it into the room just in time, for if she had arrived even a minute later, she would not have been able to locate a seat. She was grateful to be sitting, for it helped her to blend into the crowd.

Ruth noticed that Abigail Williams, Mary Walcott, Elizabeth Hubbard, Mercy Lewis, and Ann Putnam all sat in the front row of the courtroom. She saw that the girls were now sitting together in a group, so they could join together as a single unit to attack the accused.

But Ruth realized that there were additional accusers in the front row. Surprised, Ruth saw that the new accusers were not children at all, but grown women. She recognized Deliverance Hobbs and Martha Pope, both matron women, who were now joining the afflicted children to point fingers at witches.

Ruth was puzzled. She wasn't sure, but it seemed to her that just a few weeks ago, Deliverance Hobbs was also accused of witchcraft. How had the switch been made from accused to accuser?

She remembered what John Indian had told her once: "Better to accuse than to be accused." Could Deliverance Hobbs have saved herself from the gallows by turning the tables and offering herself as a witness for the prosecution?

"Hear ye, hear ye," John Hathorne bellowed, and the crowd of spectators instantly became silent at the magistrate's words. The witchcraft trial had begun.

Hathorne announced, "Today in this courtroom, a woman is hereby accused of witchcraft. The accused is Rebecca Nurse. The accused will have to prove her innocence or else be judged as guilty. Conviction means death by hanging."

Then he continued, "The court has received a petition signed by twenty-six people of Salem Village, proclaiming the virtues of Mrs. Nurse. This petition will be opposed and contested by Reverend Samuel Parris, who will bring forth evidence against Mrs. Nurse. Reverend Parris, you may address the accused."

Ruth watched as Parris rose. He strolled, almost leisurely, to the front of the courtroom until he was standing directly in front of Rebecca Nurse. Ruth was reminded that this scene eerily resembled the trial of Tituba Indian. She desperately hoped that the outcome of this trial would be different than what had happened to poor Tituba.

"Goody Nurse," Parris began. There was a collective gasp in the courtroom, because instead of Mrs., the title Goody was used.

Ruth knew that Rebecca warranted the title of higher status, and she wondered if Parris was intentionally using Goody to demean the woman sitting on the witness chair.

"Goody Nurse," Parris repeated, then asked, "have you fed your familiars today?"

Appearing stunned, Rebecca said, "What?"

"Were you examined for witches' teats?"

"I…" Rebecca stammered, "I have been examined, yes."

"You were examined by two people, am I correct? These two people were Doctor Griggs and Midwife Wilkins, correct?"

"They pulled my clothes off when I was in the dungeon," Rebecca told the courtroom. "They made me stand naked in the cold, wet dungeon. They made me take my clothes off in front of all the other poor, tormented souls in that dungeon. They held a candle to me and looked at me. They put their dirty hands on me."

"I hardly think that the hands of two skilled and practiced people are dirty. Perhaps it is your own mind that sees things as being dirty. Like sees like." Parris's voice was steady. "So you agree that two highly trained medical people examined you?"

"I was examined, yes."

"Doctor Griggs and Midwife Wilkins found an unnatural protuberance of skin within the location of your genitals. Do you deny this excrescence?"

"I can't hear you," Rebecca seemed confused. "I have trouble hearing, as I am becoming old and deaf."

"I said," Parris raised his voice, "you have a witches' teat! It was discovered by Doctor Griggs and Midwife Wilkins!"

"No!" Rebecca cried. "I have women's troubles from living in the cold and wet dungeon! I've been ailing while in prison! I have swellings all over, not just in my woman's parts, but even my knuckles are so large lately that I cannot bend them. I've been faring very poorly under such strains as I've been made to endure."

"What would you say to the fact that someone in the dungeon has come forward to report that you were seen feeding a familiar while you were imprisoned?"

"What?"

Parris repeated his question.

"Whoever said those things is a liar," Rebecca said.

"And you would certainly know about liars," Parris countered, "because Satan is your master, and he is the king of liars, is that not correct?"

"No, that is not correct."

Parris turned around to face the courtroom. He talked to Rebecca but raised his eyebrows so that the spectators could see his mocking expression. "You don't believe it is correct that Satan is the king of liars?"

"That's not what I meant," Rebecca moaned. "I meant..."

"We know what you meant," Parris interrupted.

"...that I wouldn't know about liars," she finished.

"But you didn't deny that Satan is your master."

"I scorn Satan and follow only God."

"Then why did you miss church services?" Parris turned back around to face Rebecca. "There were three, maybe four Sundays before your arrest when your place in the pews was empty. Satan will not go into a church. Satan will not step on hallowed ground, and neither will his followers. Tell this court: are you a follower of the Devil?"

"I've had illnesses," Rebecca explained. "I'm getting old, and becoming feeble as time passes. I only miss church on days that I am sick. But I never fail to pray at home."

"If you really scorned Satan, then God would have interceded weeks ago to help you. But God decided to allow you to rot in the dungeon to be punished for your sins. Isn't that because you, in reality, have scorned God? And isn't that why God scorns *you?*"

"What?"

"I said God scorns you!"

"God loves all His children," Rebecca spoke evenly but firmly, "and I am among His children. God sees into all hearts, and He knows mine is pure. I follow the Lord. I am in the Light. God will see me through this in His own good time. I cannot question His ways or His wisdom. God knows the truth—that I am no witch. My conscience is clear and clean, and I am made strong by my faith."

Around her, Ruth heard movement in the courtroom. She looked at the spectators, and was heartened to see that Rebecca's speech had made an impact upon the Villagers. The crowd began murmuring, and Ruth heard little snippets from the Villagers here and there:

"Could she be telling the truth?"

"Could this one be innocent?"

"Will God intervene on Rebecca's behalf?"

Suddenly, from her front row seat, Abigail jumped off the wooden bench and stood up. "I saw the specter of Goody Nurse take sacrament from a black man," yelled Abigail.

The Villagers made a collective gasp.

Abigail shrieked. "I saw her at midnight in my own back yard, just last night! She danced with other specters in the middle of the night. If Goody Nurse is not stopped, she will infect this whole town with Satan's evil! Last week, she sent her familiar to pinch and scratch me in the middle of the night. She sent a yellow bird to peck at me! Sometimes the evil spirits bite me when I try to sleep."

As if on cue, Mary Walcott, Mary Walcott, Elizabeth Hubbard, Mercy Lewis, and Ann Putnam, also rose to their feet.

"Goody Nurse sent an apparition to me two nights ago," Ann Putnam cried loudly for all to hear. "The ghost was in her image, so I know who sent it! She wanted me to sign a red book. It was red like blood! But I refused to sign my name to Satan's book, so she hurt me. Goody Nurse scratched and pinched me, but I still kept saying no! Finally I told her that I served the Lord, and only then did she disappear."

"Witch! Witch! Witch!" The young girls began chanting in unison, gaining in pitch until it became a frenzied screeching.

Suddenly Deliverance Hobbs and Martha Pope also stood up and joined in the ruckus. The entire group swayed their shoulders and arched their backs simultaneously. All shuddered and quaked elaborately, and waived their arms above their heads in circular motions. Their eyes rolled in their sockets and spittle formed at their mouths. A tremendous spectacle was created for the Villagers in attendance, all of which were morbidly fascinated with the demonstrations of apparent demonic possession. This was assault!

For many more minutes, the apparently afflicted group of girls and women continued their abhorrent displays of fiendish agitation. Just as in previous trials, not a person in the courtroom made any attempt to stop the frenzied demonstrations. The girls and the women continued, unrestrained by any members of the court. Ruth looked at Hathorne, and realized that once again, the magistrate seemed to be just as fascinated with this performance as was everyone else in the room.

She turned to look at Reverend Parris, and saw a smirk of satisfaction on his face.

Finally the group of bewitched girls and women seemed to tire, and slowly they decelerated their exhibitionist behavior. Gradually they grew less frantic and eventually returned to their seats.

Silence filled the small courtroom. But the effect was there; the Villagers watching the trial may have believed and sympathized with Rebecca before the outburst, but now they viewed her with malice and suspicion once again.

Unaffected by the commotion, Parris once again turned to question Rebecca Nurse. "Why did you send your specter to harm these children?"

"I did not!"

"You just heard these children. Why did you torment them?"

"I tormented no one."

"What has Satan offered you in return for the corruption of Salem Village?"

"I have never had any contact with Satan. I have been offered nothing."

"What do you say to this: when you realized that Deliverance Hobbs," and here Parris pointed at to where Hobbs was sitting in the front row, "was here to accuse you, you made a statement that you were surprised to see her? Didn't you say, and I quote, 'What is she doing here, as she is one of us?'"

"What?"

"Didn't you mean, 'She is one of us witches?'"

"No, I meant that she had been accused earlier—"

"So you felt Deliverance Hobbs was one of you witches?" Parris interrupted.

"—and I was surprised to see she is now an accuser, and not an accused."

"So," Parris was unrelenting, "you meant she is one like yourself, a witch?"

"What?"

"I said you are a witch!"

"No!" cried Rebecca. "I meant that I was surprised to see Deliverance Hobbs here in the courtroom, because I thought she was one of us prisoners, that's all! I didn't mean one of us witches, I meant one of us prisoners!"

"Oh, so *now* you explain," Parris scoffed. "But right before your trial began this morning, you were asked the same question that I just asked. And at that time, you said nothing! This morning, you didn't defend yourself! Do you admit that earlier this morning, you did not deny that you thought that Deliverance Hobbs was one of 'you' witches?"

"If I was asked that question this morning," Rebecca said, "I didn't hear it. I can't imagine not answering if I had heard it. I'm hard of hearing. I'm going deaf! So, if I was asked that question before the trial began, I didn't hear it."

"Or, this morning you heard and didn't have enough time to think of a lie!" Parris thundered. "But now you have had an hour or two to think about it, so now you have formulated a lie to tell this court, isn't that right?"

"No." Rebecca once again became calm and firm, as if resigned to a bad fate. "This is the truth: I know that Deliverance Hobbs was at one time accused of being a witch. But since that time, she has confessed and now she accuses others. Because of that, Deliverance Hobbs is now a free woman. I believe you decided that she is more valuable to you as an accuser than as another one of the accused. Who tells Deliverance Hobbs who she should accuse? You? Or John Putnam?"

The courtroom broke out in pandemonium.

"Come to order!" Hathorne bellowed, but he was unable to silence the noisy and unruly crowd. People stood up and shouted, all wanting to be heard above the others. Some began to make their way into the aisle way in order to move to the front of the courtroom, but Hathorne yelled again.

"Everyone who does not at this instant sit down and be quiet will be arrested!" the magistrate shouted.

People stopped, and began to sit back down into their seats.

But Rebecca Nurse was not finished.

"Reverend, let me ask *you* a question!" she cried out for all the spectators to hear. "Isn't it true that if I were hung, John Putnam would then obtain my land and gain the rights to my waterway?"

"Silence!" Hathorne bellowed.

"Reverend Parris, aren't you good friends with John Putnam?" Rebecca persisted.

"Woman, you'd better stop speaking such lies or else you will be hanged immediately without benefit of further trial," John Hathorne threatened.

"I'm already doomed," Rebecca said sadly.

The crowd had been quiet throughout this exchange. But suddenly there was murmuring throughout the room and Ruth saw the reason for the diversion.

Israel Porter was walking down the aisle towards the front of the courtroom.

"May I address the court?" he asked when he reached the railing.

"No! Israel Porter, you have no right to do this," Parris blustered.

Porter remained calm, and although he addressed Parris, he looked only at the judge. "Isn't this a fair trial? One which considers all evidence?"

"It is," Hathorne agreed. "I am an honest judge, and all my trials are fair, so you may speak."

"The petition proclaiming the virtuous and pious nature of Rebecca Nurse is signed by twenty-six good citizens of Salem Village. That petition also bears my signature," Porter said. "I do not take my commitment to Mrs. Nurse lightly. In fact, I have personally discussed this case with Sir William Phipps, whom everyone knows is the governor of Massachusetts."

There was movement and murmuring in the courtroom as everyone absorbed this.

"Surely you would not discount the involvement of the governor?" Porter asked. What was not added was that Hathorne's political future could be affected if an unpopular sentence was given to Rebecca now that the case had suddenly become politically sensitive.

"What was Sir Phipps' comments on the matter?" asked Hathorne. The crowd in the seats leaned forward, straining to hear.

"He said that spectral evidence should not be taken into account," Porter revealed, and there were gasps heard from the courtroom.

"What!" cried Parris. "Everyone knows that ghosts and apparitions are sent only by Satan!"

Finally Porter turned to face Parris. "That may be, but it is also a fact that Satan can send ghosts *in the likeness* of an innocent person. You said yourself that Satan is the king of liars. He can send forth a specter resembling an innocent person that might not be the innocent person. So Sir Phipps has ruled that spectral evidence should not be used in this trial—or in any trial in the commonwealth of Massachusetts."

Everyone in the courtroom appeared stunned, especially Samuel Parris.

When a few minutes passed, Hathorne asked, "So, Sir Phipps has ruled this?"

"That he has," Porter confirmed.

"What about the witches' teat?" cried Parris.

"You heard Mrs. Nurse testify that she has women's illnesses. She should be rested out of the dungeon for a day and then re-examined," Porter spoke calmly. "After all, we want the truth in this trial to come forward, don't we? Is it better to risk letting witches go free than to cause even one innocent child of God to hang?"

"We can't let witches go free!" Parris' face was scarlet.

"Well, we can't hang innocent people, either," Porter said, then turning to Hathorne, he asked, "Well, what do you say to this? Without spectral evidence, you have no cause to imprison Mrs. Nurse. After all, she has the backing of all who signed the petition. Can you ignore the testimonies of good, God-fearing Villagers?"

Hathorne appeared unhappy. "Perhaps the court should reconsider Rebecca Nurse's case. Perhaps the court should honor the petition, especially if Sir William Phipps is involved."

At those words, Abigail Williams, Mary Walcott, Elizabeth Hubbard, Mercy Lewis, and Ann Putnam all jumped to their feet and began shrieking. Deliverance Hobbs and Martha Pope joined in. The bewitched group howled and shouted in unison as they twisted their torsos and gyrated with frenzied motions.

Abigail began to speak loudly for all to hear, "Goody Nurse makes her witchcraft spells to hurt children. Will she come after *your* children? All of you—" Abigail swept her arm, pointing to all in the courtroom, "—all of you have children. Whose child will be next? Stop her! Stop Goody Nurse before *your* children are tormented by her demons!"

Ann Putnam joined in. "That's right! Are you willing to set a witch free to prey upon your children? Look at me—she is pinching me! Goody Nurse is hurting me right now!"

Mary Walcott screamed, "Look! I see a yellow bird pecking at Goody Nurse's fingers!"

Abigail chimed in. "In the rafters, the dark man is back! Goody Nurse sends her evil to torment me! And it hurts. Rebecca Nurse torments children because she wants their young souls! All of you must choose between Goody Nurse and *your very own children!*"

The group collectively began displaying their afflictions of demonic possession. Bedlam erupted in the courtroom, as the spectators began getting off their seats and joining the young bewitched girls in screaming matches.

"We must protect our children!" someone in the crowd yelled.

"Don't let witches torment our children!" cried another voice.

Abigail shouted, "All of you! Choose between this witch and your very own children!"

"Hang the witch!" someone in the courtroom crowd cried out. "Protect our children!"

Abigail Williams, Mary Walcott, Elizabeth Hubbard, Mercy Lewis, and Ann Putnam began chanting, "Hang the witch! Hang the witch! Hang the witch!"

"All of you, sit down!" John Hathorne bellowed. "I'll have order in this court!"

But nobody paid him any mind. At that point, Mary Walcott fell to the floor and began to convulse wildly.

"We'll have an answer. The touch test will be done," Hathorne suddenly announced, then pointed at a man in the second row of spectators. "You, Henry Brattle, pick up Mary Walcott and bring her to Rebecca Nurse. If Goody Nurse touches her and the child is cured of her affliction, then the evil has flowed out of the victim and back into the witch! If Mary is cured, then it is proof that Goody Nurse is indeed a witch. But if the child remains afflicted, than Goody Nurse is innocent and will be set free."

"The touch test! The touch test!" chanted the bewitched girls.

Henry Brattle lifted Mary Walcott and brought her twitching body to the front of the courtroom. He presented the child to Rebecca Nurse.

"Touch her," Hathorne commanded.

"I refuse," said Rebecca.

"Touch her, or you will be condemned," Hathorne ordered.

Resigned, Rebecca reached out to touch Mary Walcott. Suddenly the audience became deathly silent and all craned their necks to see.

The very minute that Rebecca's fingers made contact with her arm, Mary was instantly revived. Mary rolled out of Brattle's arms and stood upright. "I'm better!" she cried. "I'm cured of my affliction! The evil in my body flowed back into the witch at her touch. Rebecca Nurse is a witch!"

"There's your proof," announced Hathorne. "I sentence Rebecca Nurse to death by hanging for the crime of assault by witchcraft."

Chapter Eighteen

"There was nothing I could do for Rebecca Nurse," Ruth lamented, "nothing at all."

It was two days after the trial, and the three of them were sitting at the dining room table in the Green house. William looked at Ruth with sympathy.

Joseph told her, "It was not in your power to prevent the sentence that Mrs. Nurse was given."

"I went to the trial because I thought I could do something to help her," Ruth persisted.

"If you had spoken up in the courtroom," William pointed out, "then you'd have been caught, and you'd be back in the dungeon right now awaiting your turn to be hanged."

"I suppose you're right," Ruth sighed.

Joseph spoke to William. "On the other hand, she's right too. In Psalm 146, it says, 'Which executeth judgment for the oppressed, the Lord looseth the prisoners.' Perhaps there are times when the Good Lord could use us to help Him do His work."

"What do you mean?" William asked.

"Perhaps another rescue is in order."

"What!" cried William. "The jail is so heavily guarded now that not even a cockroach can sneak in. And no one can be bribed anymore, either."

"Yesterday Bridget Bishop was executed," Joseph said. "She was hung from the oak tree on Gallows Hill."

"Oh!" cried Ruth. Her voice caught in a sob. "Oh, I failed her."

"You did what you could," William tried to soothe her.

"Remember, your bravery saved an innocent child. Now Dorcus Good has a chance to grow up. It's not on your shoulders to carry the burden of the insanity that's surrounding Salem Village."

"The point is," Joseph continued, "that the hangings are starting. Next Saturday, Rebecca Nurse, Sarah Good, Tituba Indian, John Proctor and Elizabeth Proctor are scheduled to be executed."

"What happened to Sarah Osborne?" William asked.

"She died in the jail," Joseph informed them. "She was old and sick, and she couldn't endure the horrible conditions of the dungeon."

"Oh, that poor woman! Another person died because of this town's insanity. It's all so terrible!" Ruth cried. "What can we do about the others that are to hang on Saturday? We *must* do something to stop the hangings!"

"Maybe we can make plans for intervention," Joseph offered. "Maybe we can intercept the jail cart when the accused are transported to the hanging tree. Maybe we can do something then. I don't think we can rescue everybody condemned to die on Saturday, but we should try to save at least one more of God's children. Through us, we can help God deliver His mercy. We should try to save at least one more person."

"I'd like to rescue Rebecca Nurse and Tituba Indian most of all," Ruth spoke passionately. "I know it sounds crazy, but I feel sort of responsible for those two. I feel that Rebecca is in jail because of my father's greed, and I also feel that I should have done more during Tituba's trial on her behalf."

Then she looked at Joseph. "I've only known two ministers in all my life, Deodat Lawson and of course Samuel Parris. But you're so very different from either one of them."

"If read by someone who is afraid to look honestly within himself, the Bible can be interpreted as dire and frightful. In reality, the price for the sins of mankind has already been paid by the sacrifice of God's only Son. Satan is not powerful enough to prevail over that great sacrifice. When I'm ready to take over a pulpit," Joseph smiled, "I will preach about God's love and the goodness of His mercy. There has been far too much fear, hatred and overall darkness in Salem Village. I will teach of His shining light."

Joseph reached for a Bible that lay on the table. He opened it, and began to read: "We are of God: hereby know we the spirit of truth, and the spirit of error. Beloved, let us love one another, for love is of God."

Ruth sat quietly for a moment, deep in thought. Then she said to Joseph, "How different things would be if you were the minister of Salem Village."

"And he will be soon," William interjected, sounding determined.

Joseph laughed. "Wait a minute. For one thing, I'm only twenty-two years old, and I've never led a congregation before. I've no experience. For the other thing, Reverend Parris will never resign."

"My father is coordinating a movement of Villagers against Samuel Parris," William said. "Parris will be forced to resign. My father is recruiting the help of Sir William Phipps in this matter."

"Sir Phipps is willing to come to Salem Village to help Israel Porter?" Joseph asked incredulously.

"Not exactly," William admitted. "But he is writing a proclamation against the witch trials. The political tide is turning, and Parris will be drowned in a sea of change."

"That won't help those poor people next Saturday at the hanging tree," Ruth pointed out.

"We can help them," Joseph said. "God works through people to help people. We need to formulate a plan. Let's get to work."

The cart carrying the condemned souls moved slowly as it heaved and tilted drunkenly along the rutted country road. The five accused witches were all crammed into the single cart, a wooden vehicle that contained both a top and a bottom with bars in-between, making it resemble a crude cage of sorts. The doomed souls inside had to either sit or crouch, as the cart was not very tall, and there was barely enough room for three people, much less five that were forced to share the space.

A number of Villagers had elected to witness the executions, so there was a procession on foot following the cart. Among the Villagers walking behind the condemned strode Samuel Parris and Abigail Williams.

Off to the side of the road were dense bushes and trees. It was in those bushes that Ruth waited, hidden from the sight of the Villagers. She knew that there was strength in numbers, and was kept calm by remembering that she had William and Joseph by her side. Four other men from Salem Village, who shared her renegade ideas and wanted to come along, were also waiting with her in the bushes.

The group had two extra horses with them, with the hope that each extra horse would carry an accused witch away from Gallows Hill, rescued from execution.

Each rescuer waiting in the bushes was on top of a gentle but fast horse. Each held a pillow linen in his or her hand, with holes cut out where the eyes would be, so that they could all see once the pillow linens were put over their faces.

As the cart creaked and groaned its way up the curved road at the base of Gallows Hill, the rescuers watched from their hiding spots. Soon the cart transporting the five accused witches could go no further, because the road had minimized into a trail, too narrow and rough for anything but pedestrians to maneuver.

A burly man opened the wooden door of the jail cart and the metal hinges creaked. "Get out!" the burly man commanded and the prisoners all complied with the best of their abilities, considering that their wrists were still shackled. Their chains rattled and their eyes blinked in the sunlight as the accused witches slowly emerged from the cart. One by one they stood on the ground, dejectedly awaiting further orders, and enduring the open contempt of the crowd.

People spit, they shouted, and they threw things at the five prisoners.

A rock narrowly missed John Proctor, but none of the Village officials in attendance interceded to prevent the abuse. Instead, the burly man prodded the nearest prisoner, Tituba Indian, with a sharp stick. "All of you heathen," he ordered, "get walking."

The frailty of Rebecca Nurse became obvious when she stumbled and fell in the dirt. She couldn't get up immediately, so the burly man grabbed her hair and jerked her upright. Rebecca howled in pain, which only encouraged the crowd of spectators to shout insults and scream for violence even more openly.

"Hurt the witches!" someone in the crowd jeered. "Get revenge for what they did to our children!"

"Hang them!" someone else joined in. "Break their necks with the gallows noose!"

And from the bushes, Ruth silently wondered if she could somehow manage to rescue all of the victims of the Salem witch trials.

The plan was to rescue only Rebecca Nurse and Tituba Indian this time. But what of John Proctor, who so deeply loved his wife? And what of Elizabeth Proctor, too young to face such an untimely death? And what of Sarah Good, who may have been a beggar, but who was also the mother of a four-year-old child who needed her?

She looked at the men who were waiting with her in the dense shrubbery. Weren't there enough of them to take on the Villagers? Couldn't they rescue all of the prisoners?

But in her heart she knew she must not let her emotions get away with her. Because they had already made a plan, and any deviation of that plan could endanger themselves. If they took on one more person than they could handle, they would fail completely in their mission.

As much as she hated to admit it, they would only be rescuing two people on this day.

It broke her heart that the rest would surely hang. She thought of the other prisoners, still waiting their execution dates in the dungeon. There was nothing she could do for those people, either. Their fate would depend upon Israel Porter's success in the negotiations with Sir William Phipps.

Ruth forced herself to concentrate upon the present. The burly man seemed to take a perverted enjoyment with prodding his sharp stick into the accused witches. The man became relentless with his stabbings of the prisoners. Any outcry of pain led to more verbal displays of contempt from the crowd. It was a frenzy of hate; and everyone seemed to be out for blood.

The prisoners struggled up the hill, some ducking the sticks and stones thrown at them, others not caring if they were hit with flying debris.

All of the accused witches had been excommunicated from the church, and they were overwhelmed with the idea that they were going straight to Hell. None had any hope of being shown any mercy by the God they had loved all their lives. None had any hope that God would consider their innocence. They had been told by the church that excommunication was irrevocable. They had been taught the doctrine that if excommunicated, they were doomed to eternal suffering and total damnation, deserved or not.

Finally the entire procession of people reached the top of Gallows Hill. The strong branches of the oak tree loomed overhead, and a rope was thrown over the mightiest limb. A man dressed in somber clothes began tying the end of the heavy cord of the rope: thirteen loops over a slipknot.

"Who's to be first?" someone from the crowd asked excitedly.

"The beggar! The beggar! Hang the beggar!" someone answered.

The burly man grabbed Sarah Good by the flesh of her upper arm and pulled her to the front of the bloodthirsty crowd. "Watch the witch be sent to Hell!" he cried.

Samuel Parris stepped forward. "Witch, do you have any last words?"

Goody Good remained defiant. "I am no witch!" she shouted. "Reverend Parris, if you murder me, you will fall from grace. From my blood, yours will soon flow."

At Sarah Good's prediction of Parris' future, the crowd went wild. "Satan's words!" they cried. "Hang the witch before she hexes us all!"

A wooden ladder was thrust in front of the beggarwoman. The rope's noose was loosely placed over her head until it rested limply upon her shoulders. Goody Good still remained defiant, sneering in contempt at the crowd that had no pity or remorse.

"Get up the ladder," ordered the burly man.

"I'm not going to assist in my own murder," Goody Good hissed.

The burly man grabbed her and pushed so hard that Sarah Good was forced up three rungs. Then he took his pointed stick and savagely prodded her. The beggarwoman cried out from pain and the man grinned, shoving his stick into her legs as she was forced to continue the ascent up the ladder of death.

She reached the top of the ladder, and the burly man cried, "Secure the rope!"

The other man, who was dressed in somber clothing, pulled the rope until it was taught and tied it tightly to the tree. There would be no letting loose from the tree. The rope would do the job.

Suddenly the burly man kicked the ladder out from under the beggarwoman's feet. It tumbled over and fell to the ground.

The crowd suddenly hushed. There were no sounds; even the birds were eerily silent.

Swaying from the motion of the fall off the ladder, the body of Sarah Good swung like a pendulum, back and forth.

But death was not immediate. She was racked with convulsions as she desperately attempted to raise her arms to where the noose dug into her flesh. Her wrists still shackled with chains; Sarah Good was unable to prevent the inevitable.

She swung back and forth, jerking in the throes of death.

The crowd gawked. No one said a word. They watched intently with morbid fascination.

Ruth also watched. From her hiding place in the bushes, she was appalled at what she was seeing. Never would she have believed that anything on earth could be so awful as witnessing the hanging of Sarah Good.

But it was the beggarwoman's face that was the most horrifying. Bulging and purple from the circulation being cut off, it was a grotesque caricature of a human face. Sarah Good's eyes were practically popping from the sockets and her tongue protruded in a hideous manner.

"Why is it taking her so long to die?" Ruth whispered.

William, sitting on his horse in the shrubbery next to her, whispered back, "Because the hangman's knot slipped. It slipped to the back of the neck. When a person is hanged, usually they die instantly from a broken neck. But poor Goody Good is being strangled to death."

"Oh!" Ruth quietly sobbed.

It seemed like an eternity of time, but within minutes, the beggarwoman's struggles ceased. The momentum of her swinging slowed, and finally she just hung limply.

Sarah Good was declared dead by Reverend Parris.

The crowd continued to be subdued. They murmured instead of shouted. Perhaps this had been more than even the most bloodthirsty person would have wanted to witness. But still, no one made any efforts to stop the executions.

"Cut her down," instructed Reverend Parris. "Throw her body in the crevice on the other side of this hill. There will be no Christian burial for witches. Leave them to be scavenged by the wild animals in that rocky hole in the hill."

Ruth saw movement beside her out of the corner of her eye as William shifted his position upon his horse. "Get ready," he spoke softly to all who were waiting alongside him. "When the men guarding the prisoners take Goody Good's body away, we'll make our move."

Ruth felt the adrenaline course through her veins in anticipation of the danger to which she was about to subject herself.

But she silently told herself to be calm. This was something she knew she needed to do. She could never live with herself if she didn't try to save at least two more innocent lives.

How she wished she could save them all! But they had only

brought two extra horses.

The rope was cut from the huge oak tree and Sarah Good's body dropped quickly to the ground with a loud *thud*.

The crowd sighed collectively and seemed to move backwards just a little bit. The burly man strode over to the body lying limply on the ground and bent down over what remained of Sarah Good. He motioned for the man in somber clothes to join him and together they lifted the dead beggarwoman.

The two men began to carry the woman to the edge of the hill, where they would throw her body into the crevice.

"Now," William said, giving the signal for the daring rescue to begin.

Chapter Nineteen

She threw the pillow linen over her head as a hood, and lightly kicked the sides of the horse with her heels. The animal bolted forward, bursting out of the underbrush and leaping into the open sunlight. Through the holes cut in the hood, Ruth could see that William was at her side as she rode up the hill towards the hanging tree.

At first the Villagers didn't see the approaching rescuers, but suddenly the people realized that seven horses were galloping straight at them. With loud shouts of surprise, the Villagers scattered to get out of the way of the thundering hooves.

Ruth hung on to the saddle with everything she had. She knew that the terrain on Gallows Hill was rough and she was terrified that she could take a fall.

But she didn't change her mind. She leaned forward and rode hard.

The reins felt greasy in her hands and she realized it was from her own sweat. The disbursing crowd became a blur of colors in her peripheral vision as the Villagers scrambled to avoid being trampled. The cloth from her hood was blown by the wind and pressed against her face. The material was stifling and she felt unable to draw in the deep breaths she wanted. Her mouth was dry and she could feel her pulse racing.

William and Joseph each led one of the two extra horses, tied to their own mounts. The riderless horses followed closely behind, so that neither William nor Joseph were impeded by the additional animals.

The seven riders reached the small group of condemned prisoners who were momentarily unguarded. The rescuers simultaneously slowed their mounts and began to circle the accused witches.

Quickly William jumped off his horse and grabbed Tituba Indian. Before Tituba understood what was happening, he hoisted her into the saddle of one of the extra horses. He had to take the precious minutes to secure Tituba with the rope, because her shackled wrists would impede her ability to stay in the saddle otherwise.

But when Joseph leaped off his horse and began to grab Rebecca Nurse, she fought against his efforts.

"Don't waste your time on me!" Rebecca cried. "I'm old! Take Elizabeth Proctor instead of me. She's too young to die."

Ruth could see the burly man and the other one dressed in somber clothes running towards them from the crevice where they had thrown the body of Sarah Good. She felt a rush of panic.

"They're coming!" she yelled at Joseph. "Hurry!"

"Get on this horse!" Joseph shouted. "Rebecca, get on!"

John Proctor joined in. "You heard Mrs. Nurse! Take my wife instead! Please!"

Suddenly Samuel Parris appeared from seemingly nowhere, on foot. The minister burst into the circle of the seven rescuers. Parris held the burly man's pointed stick.

Parris began shoving the stick, trying to impale the mount of the rescuer nearest to himself, who was one of the four men from the Village. Viciously Parris stabbed the rescuer's horse with the pointed stick, spearing the animal.

The horse neighed in pain and then reared up on its hind legs. Its bit in its mouth, the horse bolted and began galloping back down the hill in the direction from which it came, taking the rescuer with it.

Meanwhile Joseph was still yelling at Rebecca. "There's no time to argue!"

"Take Elizabeth Proctor instead of me," Rebecca continued to insist, and precious time was wasted. Ruth was frantic with worry, because the burly man was almost upon them.

Parris successfully attacked another rescuer's horse, causing that animal to flee also, carrying its rider with it.

"My wife is with child!" John Proctor desperately called out to Joseph. "If she is hanged, then *two* innocent lives will be lost. Take my wife with you!"

There was no more time. The burly man was merely steps away.

Parris was once again stabbing in the air with his long, pointed stick, but this time he was aiming at Ruth's horse.

Ruth tugged at the reins and tried to turn her horse's head so the animal would get out of the way. Parris plunged the spear-like stick at Ruth's horse, but missed his target. In the momentum of the thrust, the stick became embedded in the ground

Parris tugged the stick loose, then whirled around to resume his attacks.

She pulled on the reins again, but when her horse turned this time, the pillow linen upon her head shifted. The cutouts for her eyes were no longer positioned properly, so Ruth couldn't see where Parris was standing.

She was momentarily confused and very, very frightened. What would she do if Parris stabbed her horse?

Quickly Ruth took one of her hands off the reins and used valuable seconds to position the cloth covering her head. When she could see again, she was horrified to realize that Parris was standing right in front of her horse, his arms raised in deadly aim. Ruth knew that if he shoved the stick from that position, he would spear the horse's neck and would kill the animal.

In a panic, Ruth pulled back on the reins with all her might. In confusion, her horse reared up to stand on its hind legs, its front hooves lashing out in the air. One of the horse's hooves struck Samuel Parris in the head, and the minister dropped to the ground a heap.

Oh! Ruth thought, *Did my horse kill him?*

But there was no time to wonder, because the burly man had finally reached her.

The burly man reached up, grabbing for the reins to try to stop her horse. But she managed to shove his hands away.

Glancing at the other rescuers, Ruth saw that William was back on his own horse with Tituba Indian on the extra horse that followed. She looked at Joseph, and saw that he was also on his own horse, leading Elizabeth Proctor on the horse behind him.

If they had any hope to get away, then they would all have to leave *now*.

"All ride!" cried William, as though he realized the exact same thing that Ruth was thinking. "Let's go!"

The five remaining rescuers dug their heels into their mounts, and they thundered back down Gallows Hill, leaving a scene of chaos behind.

The group had successfully rescued Tituba Indian and Elizabeth Proctor.

Weeks passed. The identity of the rescuers was never determined by the courts of Salem Town. Tituba Indian and Elizabeth Proctor were both made comfortable in the Green household.

But the hangings of accused witches continued. And Ruth received news that Samuel Parris was alive and well. So her horse hadn't killed him after all. He was still alive to do more damage to the innocent people of Salem Village.

Ruth was restless; she was continuously upset at the ongoing hangings at Gallows Hill. William tried to console her by reminding her that his father, Israel Porter, was deep in negotiations with the governor of Massachusetts to stop the murdering of innocent people.

"But what can we do in the meantime?" Ruth asked over and over again.

The answer was always the same. William told her that they had done all they could. Even Joseph agreed, and insisted that William was right.

One day, William told Ruth that his father had business in Salem Town, and was unable to make a necessary trip to Boston for an appointment with Sir William Phipps. Israel Porter had asked William and Joseph to go in his place. As the elder Greens were in the fields, it would only be herself, the Green's servant,

Elizabeth, and Tituba in the house. There were no men at home.

"Do you think you will be all right?" asked William with concern as he stood at the front door.

"Of course I'll be all right," Ruth smiled.

He looked at her. "Yes, I believe you will be. You are the bravest woman in the world."

She laughed. Then he took both of her hands in his own.

Ruth looked at their interlocked hands, then up at his face. She could see how handsome he was. He had a strong chin and a straight nose. But it was his eyes that attracted her the most; they were large, brown and deep, and framed with dark lashes.

She was sure, very sure, that she loved William Porter.

He stood there for a minute, smiling at her, and Ruth was certain that the feeling of love was returned. She could see it in his expression, and her heart leapt with joy.

"When this is all over, there will be a wedding," William told her.

But then he was gone, and Ruth turned around to join the others in the Green household.

She thought that she had better check on Elizabeth. It was around seven in the morning, and since it was now summer, the sun had already risen. She knew that Elizabeth was heavy with child, and all that the pregnant woman had endured over the previous months had taken its toll. Elizabeth was confined to her bed because she was having periodic pains.

Ruth knocked on her door. "Elizabeth, are you all right?"

The response sounded strained. "Come in."

The minute Ruth stepped inside the bedroom, she knew that Elizabeth was in trouble. The pregnant woman's hair was adhering to her skull from sweat, and her face was deathly pale. She was breathing shallowly and appeared frightened.

It was Elizabeth Proctor's first child, and by all appearances, the baby was trying to be born.

"What can I do?" Ruth didn't waste time. She knew that the men had already gone and so if anything were to be done, she would have to be the one to do it.

"Get a midwife," Elizabeth gasped. "Something's wrong."

Ruth hesitated. She knew it wasn't safe for her to ride into Salem Village. But then she made up her mind. She had to find help, because she was no midwife, and Tituba was a housemaid and not a midwife either.

"I'll get Tituba to stay with you while I'm gone," Ruth told Elizabeth, and she left the room.

After talking to Tituba, Ruth ran to the barn and saddled the brown mare that she had ridden to Rebecca Nurse's trial. She had to get help for Elizabeth.

Ruth knew that one of the Village men who had ridden with her during the Gallows Hill rescue had a wife who was a midwife. She knew she would be safe going there. The man's name was Daniel Miller, and he was part of the secret group of Villagers who attended the dissident meetings at the Green household.

As she lifted herself into the saddle, Ruth realized just how different her life had become from anything she would have ever expected. Never would she at one time have believed that she was making decisions just like a man. Her Puritan upbringing always dictated that women were to remain in the house and raise children. The women in Salem Village were taught from the time they were born that they were to marry and then obey the decisions of their husbands.

Yet here she was, making decisions of her own.

And today her decision was to find help for Elizabeth Proctor.

She left the barn door and directed her mount towards Salem Village. Ruth was trying to plan how she could reach the Miller farm without going through the Village itself. She knew what she was doing was risky but she also knew she could detour around the Village.

Although she had not been recognized during the rescue at Gallows Hill, she nonetheless understood that she was still considered to be a witch by the Villagers, and that if discovered, the jailers would capture her and throw her back into the dungeon underneath the jail.

She wanted to move quickly but not hard enough to tire her horse. After all, she would need the same horse for the return trip. She settled on a canter, and figured that pace would have to do.

When she drew closer to her destination, she chose the route that would keep her away from the boundaries of Salem Village. The last thing she wanted to do was to ride into Main Street.

But Ruth was nervous, because she knew the Miller farm was located very close to the Parris house. She was relieved when she reached the Miller farm without incident. No one stopped her! No one even saw her. She would be all right.

Ruth knocked on the door, and Daniel Miller himself answered. She explained the situation to him.

"My wife and I will ride to the Green farm immediately," Daniel assured her. "I want to do all I can for Mrs. Proctor. If we can save her and the baby, then that's two more people to survive the madness that's come over Salem Village."

With that, he summoned his wife and gathered her medical instruments. Two horses were saddled and the Millers joined Ruth to ride back to the Green household.

But Ruth only rode a very short ways when she realized that her horse seemed reluctant to proceed. Her heart sank and she felt extreme stress when it dawned on her that her horse was limping.

"Oh no!" Ruth cried. "Daniel, my horse is lame!"

He pulled his horse so that he was directly alongside of her. "Are you sure?"

"Yes," Ruth lamented.

The three riders stopped their horses. "I'll find out if the problem is in the hoof or in the leg," Daniel said as he dismounted. He picked up the brown mare's foot and looked at it closely, then announced, "There's a rock in the hoof."

"Can you dislodge it?" Ruth asked.

"No. You'll need a blacksmith to dig this rock out. It's in there pretty tight."

"What can I do? Do you have another horse I can use for this trip?"

Daniel straightened up, then hesitated a moment before he

answered. "We had a poor rye crop this year. There was some sort of fungus growing upon it. I had to sell our only other horse to raise the money we lost because of the tainted rye grain."

"Why don't you give me your horse, and you can take mine back to your farm," Ruth suggested.

"I'm sorry, but I won't leave my wife to travel without me. My wife must be my priority."

Ruth was silent as she considered this bit of news. Then she said, "Well then, you two must go on to help Elizabeth. I'll go back to your farm and wait there for your return, if it's all right with you."

Daniel shielded his eyes from the sun with his hand. Still standing on the ground, he looked up at her. "We have no servants. You'd have to be in my house all by yourself."

Ruth grinned. "Is that all you're worried about? I've been through a lot scarier things than this lately."

Daniel studied her. "Yes, you were with us at Gallows Hill, weren't you?"

"I sure was."

"Well then," Daniel told her, "go ahead and go back to my house. You'll need to lead your mare, though. You can't ride her in this condition."

"You two go help Elizabeth Proctor, and don't worry about me," Ruth said. "Go with God."

"Yes, we will," Daniel said, getting back on his mount. He and his wife turned their horses and rode off.

Sadly Ruth dismounted. She went to the head of her horse and patted its nose. "Not your fault," she crooned to the brown mare. Then she took the reins and started to walk back to the Miller farm.

But when she got there, Ruth discovered that she was not all alone at the Miller farm after all. Samuel Parris was standing on the front porch, with Abigail Williams at his side.

Chapter Twenty

Ruth dropped the reins she had been holding to lead the horse. Her first thought was, *How did he find me?*

Then she thought, *I have to get away. I have to run!*

So she turned on her heels and fled on foot, leaving her lame horse behind.

She didn't know where she intended to run. She only knew that if Parris caught her, she would wind up a dead woman.

Could she outrun him?

She heard shouts behind her as both Parris and Abigail gave chase. She didn't look behind herself, but she was hoping that they were on foot.

Her heart pounding and her throat constricted and dry, Ruth ran blindly. She could feel her legs pumping beneath her and her arms propelled back and forth. She leaned forward and gave it everything she had. She ran for her life.

But she panicked when she heard hoofbeats. She realized that Reverend Parris and Abigail weren't on foot after all, but had gotten on their horses. Ruth heard the hoofbeats rapidly getting closer. They were gaining on her.

And at that point, she knew in her heart that she would never make it. She was not going to escape.

She grit her teeth and continued to run. At least she wouldn't make it easy for them.

But her long skirts hobbled her. She was beginning to gasp for air, and the exertion was making her lightheaded. Still she continued to run, her feet trampling the tall summer grass.

And then the sounds of thundering hooves were right beside her. Parris had reached her.

Ruth knew it was all over, but still she ran.

The minister turned his horse so that he was right in front of her, blocking her. She faltered in her stride and had to slow down. Parris stopped his mount so that he could remain directly in her path.

Ruth tried to turn, but suddenly she felt herself being lifted off her feet. She struggled to get out of Parris' grasp, but he had an arm firmly wrapped around her waist as he leaned from the saddle like some sort of trick-rider.

He was stronger than she, and before Ruth could wriggle out of his hold, Parris pulled her up on his horse. He heaved her over the saddle in front of him, throwing her on her stomach so that she was lying across the front of the saddle near the horse's neck in a prone position. The saddle horn hurt and she had the wind knocked out of her.

When Ruth tried to raise herself up, Parris pushed her back down. She was lying across the horse, face down…captured.

So many emotions passed through Ruth as she was forced to lay prone across Parris's horse. She experienced pain from the saddle horn, embarrassment at being draped practically across the minister's lap, dread of her immediate future; but mostly she felt fear.

She was juggled and bumped during the ride, but at least Parris kept his horse to a walk. She hoped they weren't going to travel very far.

And they didn't. She was taken back to the Parris household, where everything had begun. It had begun there, and now it would end there.

The minister reined his horse to a stop at the barn, then said to Ruth, "I'll let you up. But if you try to run, things will be much worse for you than they already are. So don't run."

Resigned to her fate, Ruth tried to slip off the horse, feet first. Surprisingly, Parris helped her down, and she landed safely on the ground. She straightened up, and realized that she was very stiff and sore from lying across the horse.

Abigail had been riding sidesaddle, and dismounted also. She began to lead her horse into the Parris barn, but first stopped in front of Ruth.

"I can't wait to see you die," Abigail spat out, then disappeared into the barn with her horse.

When Abigail was gone, Ruth turned to Parris. "You can't really believe I'm a witch," she tried to reason with him.

"As God is my witness," Parris said, "I *do* believe."

"What are you going to do with me?"

"You'll be locked in Tituba's old room. Abigail will watch you," Parris replied. "I'm going to go fetch the jail cart. I will petition the court for your hanging to occur immediately."

With that, Parris lifted the reins over the horses head, then draped them on the ground. Like many horses, this one was trained that if the reins were dangling on the ground, it meant to stay put.

When Abigail came back out of the barn, the minister said, "Let's go into the house."

Ruth knew she couldn't run. She knew that Reverend Parris would be faster than she could ever be. She felt numb as she walked towards the house. Her situation seemed so unreal. It was as though she was watching it unfold through someone else's eyes. She thought, *This can't be happening to me. I must be asleep, and having a nightmare. Or maybe I have Saint Anthony's Fire again and don't know it.*

But she knew it was no dream. She knew it was no illnesss.

It was real.

They reached the heavy, wooden back door of the kitchen. When Ruth entered, she was overwhelmed with memories and none of them good. She remembered how awful it had been to live in the Parris household. When she first moved in, Ruth had been very naïve.

Now she realized that the Parris household had always been a place of malevolence. She had grown up almost overnight while living there, as a means of self-protection.

They went up the main staircase, and for the first time, Ruth saw the room where Tituba had once been confined after being accused of witchcraft. It was a barren room that contained only a small, single bed. The room contained nothing else, not even a table or an armoire.

"Stay here and guard the witch," Parris instructed Abigail. He stroked his niece's hair for a moment and looked at her fondly. "I'll be back with a chair for you. I'm also going to bring a loaded musket. If Ruth tries to escape, shoot her."

Parris left the room and Abigail turned to Ruth. "Sit on the bed. I'm in charge now. You'd better listen to me."

Ruth sat on the bed, then looked at the girl, who remained standing because she had no chair. Abigail's small dark eyes gleamed maliciously.

"You don't have to do this," Ruth said.

"I don't have to do anything I don't want to do," Abigail sniffed, "but I want to do this very much."

Ruth tried to reason with her. "Abigail, listen. You've been raised all your life in a house where the Bible has been read. You know in your heart that this is wrong. You are accusing innocent people. You are judging people here on earth, but in the long run, God will be the judge of you. Is this what you want God to consider when deciding His judgment in Heaven? You can stop all of this now and repent. God will forgive you if you stop now. Tell your uncle the truth."

"Don't give me any of that," Abigail sneered. "My uncle is a man of God. He ought to know more than you what's right and what's wrong, and Uncle Parris thinks you should die for your sins."

"But Abigail," Ruth persisted, "you were the one who started this. Your uncle is only reacting to what you told him. I understand that at one time, you were lonely, and now you are practically famous in Salem Village. That's why you started this whole witchcraft hysteria, so that people would pay attention to you. But underneath, I think you know right from wrong. Do the right thing and stop all of this."

"My uncle loves me now," Abigail said. "That's the most important thing. Plus, I have given Uncle Parris status in this

Village. These days, people respect him. People look to him with gratitude because they think he saves their children from Satan. That's all I care about."

"Abigail, please think this though," Ruth began, but at that moment, the door opened again and Parris reappeared with both a chair and a gun, so Ruth said no more.

"Remember," Parris instructed Abigail while he glared his contempt at Ruth, "if the witch tries anything, shoot her."

And he left the room.

"Abigail—" Ruth tried again.

"Oh shut up!" Abigail interrupted, shouting in obvious anger and waving the musket. "You were born into money. You think you are so high-and-mighty! But look at me! My father is dead and my mother ran off to who knows where. Nobody wanted me! But Uncle Parris wants me now. So you can just shut your mouth. I'm sick of people like you—people who had everything all their lives while I had nothing. Everyone hated me before now! But I'll get my revenge, and you'll get your comeuppance, all at the same time."

Ruth was suddenly afraid that Abigail would shoot her and lie to Parris that it was because of an escape attempt. So Ruth decided to speak no more, and waited silently on the bed.

Eventually Parris came back. "The jail cart is waiting outside," he informed Ruth. "Get in it."

Ruth went down the main staircase and out the front door. She was surprised to discover that John Hathorne was sitting on a horse, waiting for her outside. Hathorne looked at her, then pointed to the jail cart.

Minutes later, Ruth found herself inside the wooden structure. She sat, smoothing her skirts around her. Even though she was in a sitting position, Ruth had to lean forward to avoid the low ceiling of the jail cart.

The driver sat up in a little seat on top. Underneath the driver, the cart had sturdy wooden bars on all sides, and it was hitched to a large draft horse. The horse moved forward and the jail cart pitched and heaved down the dirt road, its wooden joints groaning and creaking.

Hathorne, Parris, and Abigail rode their horses alongside the cart.

Ruth felt both dejected and afraid. Her bad feelings intensified when she realized that the jail cart in which she was riding passed Salem Village and kept going.

They were taking her directly to Gallows Hill!

If she was afraid before, she was terrified now. She vividly remembered watching Sarah Good die. She couldn't imagine suffering so horribly like Goody Good. She was so scared that she felt physically ill.

She suddenly realized that since Hathorne was present, it meant she had already been sentenced. There would be no trial. There would only be an execution.

The jail cart groaned and creaked up the rough terrain of Gallows Hill. Soon it could go no further, and the driver dismounted to open the wooden cage door.

Ruth recognized the burly man from Sarah Good's hanging.

"Get out, Witch," the man said.

"Watch her, Henry," Parris said. "Don't let her cast any spells."

So the burly man's name was Henry. It was a common name, and she felt it was an odd name for an executioner. She would have expected something more sinister.

Ruth looked at Henry, but said nothing as she climbed out of the jail cart. Once her feet were on the ground, she tried to straighten up, but she was still stiff and sore from her prone-position ride across Parris' horse.

"Walk, or I'll stab you with my stick," threatened Henry.

Ruth knew she had no options. She began to climb Gallows Hill on foot, with Henry, Hathorne, Parris, and Abigail following closely behind.

The massive oak tree loomed in front of her; a solitary silhouette on the hilltop. From the biggest limb dangled a hanging rope. A noose with a slip knot had already been tied in anticipation of yet another victim. The ladder leaned against the tree trunk.

Ruth felt faint. She realized that she would never see another sunrise, never taste sweet honey on freshly baked wheat bread. She would never marry William Porter or bear his children. In fact, she would never see William Porter ever again.

"You have been excommunicated from the church," Parris told her as he stopped at the base of the hanging tree. "Witch, do you wish to confess?"

"I…." Ruth trailed off. Her knees didn't seem to be able to support her body anymore. They felt like liquid, and she couldn't seem to stand up with any amount of stability.

Suddenly she heard hoofbeats, lots of them. Ruth looked down Gallows Hill, and saw eight riders coming at them at a fast and furious pace.

"Hurry!" cried Abigail. "Hang the witch!"

"Go ahead, hang her," Parris commanded Henry.

Henry fumbled with the ladder, but in his attempts to try to set it up quickly, he dropped it on the ground.

"Fool!" exclaimed Parris. He pushed Henry aside and grabbed the ladder himself.

"Hang her!" Abigail shouted.

Quickly Parris set up the ladder. He grabbed at the rope that dangled from the limb of the oak tree.

Henry seized Ruth's shoulder in his hands and shoved her at the ladder. He took the rope from Parris and tried to slip the noose over Ruth's head. She twisted and turned in a desperate attempt to squirm out of his grasp. Henry was a big man, almost fat, and he was puffing from the exertion. He was slow in his reactions, and Ruth took advantage of that.

She kicked him in the knee.

Henry cried out, but let go of Ruth. She whirled on her heels and started running down Gallows Hill towards the oncoming riders. They were very close now and she recognized most of them.

One of the riders was William! He had come for her.

Others she recognized to be Joseph Green and Israel Porter.

They stopped when they reached Ruth. William said, "Get on the horse behind me. We're going up the hill."

"I've got to get out of here!" Ruth protested. "I want to go down the hill, not up."

"Trust me," he told her.

"I'll always trust you."

William held out his hand and helped Ruth climb on his horse. She sat behind him and was apprehensive when the group of riders rode towards the hanging tree and not away from it. But William had told her to trust him.

The eight riders approached Hathorne, Parris, Henry, and Abigail, and stopped.

"Israel Porter," Parris blustered, "you have no right to be here. I have permission from the court for this hanging. Ruth Putnam has been convicted and we are carrying out her sentence."

"That's right," John Hathorne joined in. "Ruth Putnam is sentenced to die for the crime of witchcraft."

"Not so fast," Israel Porter said. He dismounted from his horse and stood directly in front of Parris and Hathorne. The seven other riders remained on their horses and watched.

"How dare you interrupt this legal proceeding!" Parris shouted.

"Before you think that this proceeding is legal," Porter said, "you had better take a look at the document I've brought. It's signed by the governor of Massachusetts."

Hathorne's jaw dropped open. "You have a document signed by Sir William Phipps?"

"It's a proclamation, actually. It prohibits any more hangings for witchcraft."

Suddenly Abigail shouted, "No! Don't believe him! It's a forgery!"

Porter looked at Parris, a surprised expression on his face. "You'd better control your niece."

"Abigail, we need to look at this proclamation," Parris told her.

Abigail jumped in front of Israel Porter. "No! You're lying! You just want to cause trouble for my uncle!"

"What?" Porter looked at Abigail as though seeing her for the first time.

Parris stepped towards his niece. "Abigail, this is not the time, nor the place."

"But can't you see what they're doing?" she persisted. "Israel Porter always gets what he wants because he's rich. And now he's going to undo everything I have worked so hard to do for you. Can't you see what I've done for you, Uncle Parris? You can't let Israel Porter take it away."

Parris raised his voice. "Abigail, stop this right now!"

"No I won't stop," she continued. "I did it all for you, Uncle Parris. I made up all those stories for you. I wanted the Villagers to respect you. And now they do! All the Villagers want you to save their children. They *like* you!"

"Stop it!" Parris was shouting now. "You don't know what you're saying!"

"Let her talk," Porter said.

"That's right, I *will* talk!" Abigail's voice held venom.

Israel Porter turned to the child and prompted, "Go ahead and tell me. Judge Hathorne is listening, aren't you, John?"

Abigail glared at Porter. "You think you're so high-and-mighty. You're one of those people who always hated me. Everyone hated me. You think you're so smart? I fooled you! I fooled more people than you, even. I fooled the whole Village! I'm important now! I'm so important that it's up to me whether people live or die."

"Young lady," Hathorne growled, "I find it very hard to believe what you are saying. Are you telling the truth?"

"Maybe I am and maybe I'm not," Abigail said. "But you're not sure, are you?"

"This is no time for games," Parris said. "I command you to tell the truth."

"Okay, I will tell the truth. Everything I said is true," she turned to Parris. "But Uncle, I did it all for you! I love you! I wanted you to notice me."

Ruth heard intakes of breath as the people around her gasped. But in contrast, she felt calm, almost jubilant. The truth was finally being told, after all this time.

But how many lives were lost because of lies? For the dead, the truth had come too late.

"Abigail—" Parris began, but was interrupted.

Hathorne jumped in. "What about the symptoms of demonic possession? I witnessed witchcraft spells on the children with my very own eyes!"

For the first time, William spoke up. "It wasn't witchcraft. It was Saint Anthony's Fire. The children had the Saint Anthony's Fire sickness."

More gasps came at this revelation.

"John, can it be true?" Parris asked Hathorne.

"Well," Hathorne spoke slowly, "I've heard of such a sickness. They say it comes from eating bad grain."

"The rye grain!" Parris exclaimed. "It was tainted. But Saint Anthony's Fire—could such a thing possibly exist?"

"I have heard it to be true," William assured him.

"But the children saw apparitions," Hathorne reminded everyone. "The witches sent ghosts to hurt them in the night."

Israel Porter said icily, "Abigail just said that she made it all up."

Hathorne looked at Abigail. "Child, do you realize what you've done?"

"All of the people who were hanged hated me," Abigail spat out.

"But what about the other children who were bewitched?" Hathorne continued to question Abigail. "Surely not *all* of the children were lying."

Israel Porter spoke before Abigail had a chance to answer. "Some of the children wanted attention just as much as Abigail. Children are always made to obey their elders. But think about it—those children who accused witches were able to control adults. That must have been quite a heady experience, to have turned the tables so effectively where a situation was created where adults obeyed children. It must have made the children feel powerful."

"Still, not all the children were lying," William added, still seated on his horse with Ruth behind him. "Some of the children were obeying the directions given to them by their parents. I strongly suspect, for example, that Ann Putnam was ordered to accuse poor Rebecca Nurse of witchcraft. Rebecca had property that others wanted. It's my belief that once this witchcraft hysteria gained momentum, some people saw the situation as an opportunity for a land grab."

Hathorne looked at Porter. "The proclamation signed by Sir William Phipps—what does it say?"

Israel Porter cleared his throat and read:

> *It is hereby deemed that evidence used against any person accused of witchcraft cannot be of a spectral nature; and other evidence must be as clear and concise as with any capital case. It is hereby deemed that any accused person must have legal representation for a rejoinder. It is hereby deemed that the witchcraft trials in Salem Village were not held in a just manner; and therefore all persons who are imprisoned solely on the determination of those trials shall be set free, with the provision that payment of all prison fees shall be made.*

All were quiet while the contents of the proclamation were absorbed.

Then John Hathorne spoke. "Reverend, take your niece home."

Chapter Twenty-One

Ruth and William made plans to be married. They would recite their wedding vows in front of the new minister of Salem Village—Reverend Joseph Green.

Since the Puritan customs were to keep things simple and without embellishment, Ruth knew her wedding would be a quiet affair, but she was grateful for it at all. She was allowed to marry the man she loved, and not forced into a union decided by her parents.

She chose her best gown, and wore it as she stood in the Green's living room. William looked at her with his deep brown eyes, and she could see the joy reflected there. She hoped that joy was mirrored in her own eyes as she took his hand in front of Reverend Green.

When she was pronounced a wife, the small crowd that attended burst into life. They rushed to the table that held the spiced hard cider called sack-posset and poured drinks for all.

She remembered what William had once said to her, seemingly so long ago.

"I don't think a barn is good enough for you," he had told her. "But there will be another place for us, and when we are married, we will finish what we started."

And that night…later that night…

William smelled like leather, warm leather, and she leaned into him as he held her near the bed in the dark room. They were both standing and he whispered into her ear, "Finally the time is right."

He kissed her and his lips pressed upon hers with a circular motion. He parted her lips with his tongue and she was shocked but intrigued. She savored the feeling of his tongue exploring her mouth, and he tasted of cider, a heady, pleasant taste.

Slowly he backed her up until she stood against the bed, then he lowered her down upon it. He sat next to her and began kissing her neck. He untied the bonnet sting from under her chin, and her hat was freed from her head. He dismissed it to the floor.

He ran his hand through her thick hair, loosening it until the band that tied it became undone and also fell to the floor. Ruth's long hair tumbled around her shoulders, freed from restraint.

He kissed her lips again, and she could feel his hand against her throat as he undid the button there. She felt the material of her gown parting at her throat, and suddenly his lips were on her neck, and she could feel his warm breath upon her skin.

In a smooth gliding motion, William lowered Ruth until she lay prone upon the bed. He continued unbuttoning her gown, and pushed it aside. He slowly slid her undergarment down her chest, and her breasts were liberated and bare. He put his mouth on her nipples and nibbled at them, and Ruth gasped at the stimulation his actions created deep within her.

He continued to slide her undergarment over her stomach, over her thighs, over her feet. He discarded it upon the floor.

She lay naked on the bed. She felt beautiful.

William got up from the bed, removed his own clothes, and stood naked next to the bed. She knew he could see her in the moonlight that streamed through the window's curtains. "I'm admiring you," he told her.

"Come to me," she whispered.

He lay down on the bed next to her. He stroked her body with his fingers, a light touch yet it was firm enough not to tickle. She knew he felt her curves and his fingers lingered on her belly, then traveled below it.

And when William moved to lie on top of her, to mount her, Ruth knew that this had indeed been worth the wait.

Chapter Twenty-Two

In November, Abigail Williams was walking on Main Street when an elderly woman shoved her while passing by, and almost knocked the child down.

Abigail, infuriated by the slight, suddenly cried, "That old woman is a witch! I've seen her dancing outside my window at midnight! She collects poppet dolls and sticks pins in them to hurt children! She's pinching me! Stop her!"

But the Villagers walking down Main Street completely ignored Abigail and continued on their way, not even glancing at her.

After a few minutes of standing alone in the street, Abigail silently continued on her way, too.

About the Author

While most people go to Disneyland while in Southern California, Jeani Rector went to the Fangoria Weekend of Horror there instead. She grew up watching the Bob Wilkins Creature Feature on television and lived in a house that had the walls covered with framed Universal Monsters posters. It is all in good fun and actually, most people who know Jeani personally are of the opinion that she is a very normal person. She just writes abnormal stories. Doesn't everybody?

Jeani Rector is the founder and editor of The Horror Zine and has had her stories featured in magazines such as *Aphelion, Midnight Street, Strange Weird and Wonderful, Dark River Press, Macabre Cadaver, Ax Wound, Horrormasters, Morbid Outlook, Horror in Words, Black Petals, 63Channels, Death Head Grin, Hackwriters, Bewildering Stories, Ultraverse,* and others.

The Horror Zine Books also offers another work of historical fiction written by Jeani Rector.

PESTILENCE:
A MEDIEVAL TALE OF PLAGUE

Available on Amazon now.

PESTILENCE:
A MEDIEVAL TALE OF PLAGUE

PESTILENCE: A MEDIEVAL TALE OF PLAGUE is historic fiction, delving into a first-person account of life during the European plague years of 1346-1350. Today there are many end-of-the-world tales, but the bubonic plague pandemic in the 14th Century is the original apocalypse story.

"A very well-researched book full of facts about that time, how people lived, and the disease itself, yet it tells the story at an exciting pace."
— Larry Green, *Death Head Grin Magazine*

Made in United States
North Haven, CT
15 October 2022